The Green Lantern
& other stories

The Green Lantern

& Other Stories

by

Ariel Smart

Fithian Press
Santa Barbara • 1999

Printed in Canada

Design and typography by Jim Cook

Published by Fithian Press, a division of Daniel & Daniel, Publishers, Inc.,
Post Office Box 1525, Santa Barbara, California 93102

"Hunter" was first published in *Love and Sex in the 21st Century* (New Mexico University, 1988).

LIBRARY OF CONGRESS CATALOGING IN PUBLICATION DATA

Smart, Ariel, (date)
The Green Lantern and other stories / by Ariel Smart.
p. cm.
ISBN 1-56474-271-7 (alk. paper)
1. California – Social life and customs – Fiction.
2. Deserts – California – Fiction. I. Title.
PS3569.M373G74 1999
813'.54—DC21

98-19963
CIP

The Green Lantern
11

The Bridge Players
19

Hunter
29

The Turtle
41

Jersey Joe Versus the Rock
50

Posing
56

Vincent
66

Raccoon
79

Emily
93

Mud and Strawberries
96

The Wedding Dress
101

To my husband, Gordon Smart,
for his support and encouragement

To my writing group:
Claire Braz-Valentine, Facilitator
Ann Reh
N. Jesse Ryan
Andrea Sanelli
Mary Ann Savage
Janie Trainor
Nancy Wambach

and to my teacher,
Mary Jane Moffat

The Green Lantern

& other stories

The Green Lantern

In the vast agricultural region of Southern California's Imperial Valley were Reese's Valentine Trailer Park and, across the highway, Harper's Green Lantern Motel. The latter was owned and operated by Frank Harper, whose young wife had been unhappy in their life in the desert, and one day took a train to New York to visit her family and never returned. After the loss of his wife and in his grief, Frank Harper turned his attention to the care of their daughter, Delia.

In the years that followed his wife's departure, Frank Harper became moody and nervous, fretful about keeping a watchful eye over his daughter, and occupied with his livelihood. There was always a leaking toilet to fix, or a cabinet to reface, or new linoleum to lay in one of the cabins, and the perpetual problem of keeping the units rented. He was taciturn by nature, and he usually spoke only when necessary, and then in a loud, bass voice. He was at ease with a baseball, hammer, and rifle, and had an acquired ease with a comb.

This Sunday morning he sat in his kitchenette, wielding his fine-toothed comb. Nine-year-old Delia stood before him, turning as he directed so that he could work the snarls from her brown hair. Frank was preparing to give her the grave sermon he periodically delivered about perils waiting for her close by. After his wife's departure, he always expected the worst.

He lowered his voice almost a full octave, and declaimed his commandments to her. "First of all: don't go into anybody's cabin. There isn't any reason at all for you to go into any cabin but ours. Cabin Number 1. Not 2. Not 3. Not 4. All the other cabins, 2 through 10, are off limits. Does that make sense?"

Delia nodded her head in agreement, tugging against the hank of hair he was working on.

"Not Number 4," he emphasized. "Now stay still."

She squirmed and drew in her breath. Only last week her father had caught her just as she was about to go into Number 4 with her ten-year-old playmate, Hollis Crow, who lived there with his mother, father, and stepsister. That day, his family had been working in the sugar beet fields, and Delia and Hollis were going to go into the cabin only long enough to get a snack. Frank Harper had warned her then and there that if he found her in the Crow cabin again, she couldn't play with Hollis anymore.

Frank drew his comb down the center of her head, making a sharp part. "Remember what I'm telling you. For your own good."

"I'll remember." She tried to act attentive.

He gestured with his comb out the window. There, behind the Green Lantern's cabins and attached carports, lay acre upon acre of fields brought into harvest by the water engineered from the intricate Colorado River irrigation system. Season by season father and daughter had observed one crop after another coming into cultivation. Winter's shadowy green spinach, variegated green and red leaves of young beets, and ferny tops of carrots were followed by early spring's golden blossoms, and then summer's ripeness, melons of all varieties and hues: watermelon, casaba, Persian, Sharlyn, ambrosia, cantaloupe, muskmelon, cranshaw, and honeydew.

Frank divided the hair on one side of her head into three sections, and began working his long fingers and big knuckles in the pattern that would braid these sections together. "Stay out of the irrigation ditches. The current's deep and fast. Do you want to be drowned like a wet rat?"

Delia looked down at her bare feet on the cool green linoleum. She wondered if he had seen mud between her toes yesterday. Having been partly heedful of her father's warnings, she'd never actually gone into the ditch. She did like to play along the banks with the migrant farmworkers' children, whose parents sometimes rented cabins at the Green Lantern and worked in the fields or packing houses in nearby El Centro.

Delia heard a snapping sound near her ear as her father wrapped a red rubber band around the end of her finished braid. Then he took her hand protectively in his and led her out of the door to the front step, which faced the highway. Cars swished by going in the direction of El Centro. Dust swirled in the dry air and a yellow Caterpillar tractor crawled into the driveway of Reese's Valentine Trailer park to let a truck pass. "Don't you cross that highway. Don't even play near it. Don't try going over to the trailer park. 'Sides, I've seen people dump dogs off on the side of the road. They can get rabid and bite you."

Frank paused and drew from his back pocket a clean white cotton handkerchief. He mopped his perspiring brow, and then slipped the wet cloth through his belt loop. "Last but not least, stay off the railroad tracks. Hobos and derelicts live in jungles by the overpass. If one grabs at you, you run like hell. Run to me. I'll catch the son-of-a-bitch and stick my revolver in his pig-gut. I'll kill the derelict that ever touches you."

He looked at Delia. "If you will obey me, you are free to go play now. I've got to find Hollis. I promised to do a little target shooting with him."

Delia nodded. At first she trailed behind her father. As was usual for a Sunday afternoon, the itinerant woman tenants at the Green Lantern kept to their cabins, and their men joined each other in small groups to josh and smoke behind the motel dump in the shade cast by the beefwood trees, scrubby evergreens native to the desert. The men guzzled beer and lined up the empty bottles to use as targets.

For a time, on that particular Sunday, Delia observed her father and Hollis, who had recently acquired a .22 bolt Marlin, standing side by side, firing their rifles by turn at empty beer cans set at a distance from them.

Delia soon became bored as a mere spectator to her father's and Hollis' gunplay, a listener to the booming reports of their shots. The dust and heat and sulfuric smell irritated her eyes, nose, and throat. Then, too, the rusty cans, the broken bits and pieces of appliances and rubble scattered here and there, the discarded engine parts and tires lying about the dump, and the salty feel of dry alkaline soil under her feet were in sordid contrast to the fresh irrigated fields that spread out close by, just beyond the barbed-wire fencing.

She straddled over a loosened part of the fencing and took to the fields, and, in a high phantasy of being in companionship with Black Beauty, Ginger, Duchess, and the dappled-gray pony, Merrylegs, she galloped away with them through beds of golden blossoms full of nectar-sucking honeybees, white squash moths, and now and again, a monarch butterfly on fluttered wing from the grove of eucalyptus windbreakers that surrounded the northernmost boundary of cultivated land.

She listened to the sounds of the evasive cicada, and followed the meanderings of a silky-skinned red garter snake with a beaded turquoise stripe extending the length of his slender back, losing sight of him after he paused, his colors glittering in the sun, then flowed into a crack in the broken earth.

Delia ran deeper and deeper into the fields until the sound of gun reports was muffled by distance, and, though she could see still the outline of the beefwood trees, she could no longer distinguish individual figures.

In the fields of summer, the once-slim, blade-like green grasshoppers had aged and browned and flattened. They crawled on long, horny legs, carrying before them monstrous heads and bulging, lidless eyes. Every once in a while they became airborne and whirred up in the dry air and plunked down in the dust or fell heavily on a squash vine. She stopped skipping and picked up a grasshopper. His armor-clad body felt hot and scratchy like sandpaper. His mouth dripped a sticky liquid on her hand that resembled burnt-umber chewing tobacco juice. She thrust him away from her in the brush. His spit left an ugly yellow stain on a puffed sleeve of her blue pinafore.

Delia squatted down to pee near the green, rough leaves of a squash bed. She pulled down her pink panties with the word "Sunday" embroidered on them. The stream of water made a dusty steam on the earth, and some of the warm spray rebounded on her tanned legs. A red and black-dotted

ladybird lit on her hand and trekked like a tickle down her bare forearm. She chanted,

"Ladybird, ladybird, fly away home:
Your house is on fire;
Your children will burn."

The sound of her thin voice in wide-open space surprised her, and she became aware of a scent of sweet, weedy smoke in the dry air, as she tugged her underpants up quickly and clumsily. In a simultaneous, instinctive movement, she rose to a full standing position.

Someone was watching her, a strange man. Had he come into the field from the thicket of eucalyptus near the highway, she wondered?

As suddenly as he had appeared, he stood and faced her a short distance away. She could see dried yellow mud caked on his leather work boots as he leaned up against an embankment of an irrigation ditch. He was shirtless, stout and burly. His trouser pants hung down below the beltline and exposed his naval and a hairless belly as white as a silverfish. A dirty, wet red bandana dangled from his neck.

He had fixed his eyes on her, and he looked at her hard without seeming to blink. His mouth stretched into a thin, dark line, closed and cunning.

He dropped a burning cigarette butt to the ground, and, moving his hand away from the support of the embankment, stepped toward her. She saw the black border of his bandana closely now. From forehead to throat down to his chest he was lathered in grimy perspiration. His hair hung down loosely to his shoulders, matted and tangled.

He came close enough to reach out and touch her, and

she could smell urine on his clothes and the odor of his sweaty flesh.

At first, his advance toward her caused her to stiffen and feel small, cornered by fear as if a closet door had clicked shut, leaving her suffocating within a hot space. She felt her breath catch. Her toes numb, and she couldn't manage to wiggle and waken them to activity.

"Girlee," the stranger called out, exposing the black hole of his mouth and yellow popcorn teeth with two front ones missing.

He moved his hand down toward his groin and the zipper of his pants.

"I wanna give you something."

The strange sound of his voice in the dusty air startled her and roused her to a panic of action. *Run to me*, her father had told her.

She plunged headlong away from the shirtless stranger and ran zigzag over the ridges of the cultivated field. Dirt clods broke up at her feet. She thought she heard a tread and shuffle of boots behind her, but after a time these dissolved into the thumping of her own heartbeat resounding in her eardrums. She never stopped nor glanced back. The tumbleweed burrs nettled her bare feet, but she ran on in a blind heat toward the line of beefwood trees, the defined boundary of the autocourt.

The sun glared unmercifully on her head. Dirt clods broke up at her feet. Her eyes smarted, and lungs ached.

Then she heard her father hollering into the field.

"Delia. Delia. Delia."

He stressed "Dee" like a long, piercing "E"-pitched whistle. His voice stretched out to her like a lifeline to safety.

Soon after she heard her father's call, the balls of her feet touched familiar cracked, dry-baked alkaline soil. She faced barbed wire, and she crawled through an opening under the fencing, and found herself again on the property of the auto-court.

She looked back at the melon fields. Acres and acres of mute leaves winnowed in an empty and oblivious yellowing desert.

"So there you are. Not a minute too soon. I was just about to go looking for you. Wasn't I Hollis?" Frank Harper said.

She noticed that her father and Hollis had rigged up a wire like a makeshift clothesline between two beefwood trees and had hung upside down from it a pair of white cottontail rabbits they had shot. Man and boy, each of them, worked with a knife on a rabbit, slickering away pink flesh from white fur.

Delia's father peeled down his rabbit's pelt. It fell in a white tube at his feet.

The Bridge Players

Every February two childless, middle-aged couples, the Meyers and the Fishbeins, drove down together from Los Angeles and rented cottage units at Frank Harper's Green Lantern Motel for two weeks following Valentine's Day. During the rest of the year, Irving Meyers and Harvey Fishbein were buyers of men's furnishings for a chain of large Western-based department stores in Los Angeles. Alvie Meyers and her sister Trudy Fishbein owned a florist shop, The Desert Flower, near Seventh and Broadway.

When they arrived at the motel the first day of their stay, it was Mrs. Fishbein who sat at the wheel of a big, royal-blue, chrome-rimmed Buick, its engine hot, the windshield and radiator grill besmirched, smeared with crushed flying insects' wings and bits of legs. She let her brother-in-law, Irv Meyers, off at the manager's unit for check-in and keys and then swung the car past the sign in the office window, which read in bold, black lettering: No Dogs. Then she maneuvered the boat-like vehicle towards the group's favorite cabins, Number 9 and 10.

They've got the dog with them, Delia thought. She gazed uneasily at the pile of stones her father kept outside his office door. She knew their use. She had seen her father grab up rocks from that heap and hurl them one at a time at any stray dog that had the misfortune of coming into the motel grounds. *Why does he have to be so mean to them?* She wondered, *Why couldn't I have a dog?*

At suppertime the night before, she had set aside the book she was reading, *Lad, A Dog*, and turned to her father and asked him once again if she could have a dog.

"Why won't you let me have a dog? I'd take good care of him. I promise."

She held up the book and pointed to its cover illustration showing a noble, sedate collie, aristocratic in bearing. "See, Dad, Albert Payson Terhune's dog, Lad, doesn't have fleas. He rescues people in trouble."

Frank Harper looked sharply at his daughter, and frown lines appeared on his forehead. "I don't give a damn about Mr. Terhune. Just bring a filthy dog around. I'll run him off before you can say jackass," he warned.

The Meyers always came accompanied by their tawny-brown Mexican Chihuahua, "Baby," whose existence at the motel proper Frank Harper chose to ignore. When eight-year-old Delia asked her father why the Meyers could keep a dog in their cabin, while she was not allowed to, he retorted sharply to her question, "That's my business."

S'not fair. S'not fair. None of your beeswax, Delia thought, overhearing bits and pieces of her father's and Mr. Meyer's conversation in the motel office. They discussed business. *They talk beeswax. Dog days*, her father said. Every business downtown is going belly up.

"Downtown L.A.'s dead," Irv Meyers said. "We're hurting. Who can afford ordering flowers at the gals' Desert Flower? The action's in the suburbs. Shopping malls. Broadway and Seventh? Ghost walks. Haggerty's out. Sherman Clay's out.

Out. Out. Who'd of believed this for the sixties? Fox's boarded up. Marquee reads: CLOSED UNTIL FURTHER NOTICE. Some picture! Bullock's, Broadway, May Company, all moving out to the suburbs. My business has gone to hell. How 'bout you?"

"Same here. Dead or groaning. Chris' sakes, I'm on the wrong side of the desert," Frank Harper said. "Development's at the Salton Sea. Big time! That's where resort tourist trade is."

"People are paying good money to be about 235 feet, give or take, below sea level?"

"Yep. By sixty-nine, they'll be nothn' here."

"I'm thinking Alvie and I'll have to go out to Palm Springs—if she's better. And we ain't spring chickens. Say, Frank, why don't you stop over at our cottage this evening for margaritas?"

"Maybe. Tomorrow's a school day for Delia. I've got to see she gets started on her long division. Her teacher kept her after school yesterday. Caught her cheating."

"She's in fourth grade already, isn't she? Hard to believe!" Irv Meyers said putting a fine, well-manicured finger to his mouth "just so," revealing his left pinky finger encircled in a jaunty ring set with gem stones of purple amethyst. "I'll just bet she's a good little scholar," he said, standing near the open door of the motel office looking in Delia's direction as she rode her bicycle back and forth down the long driveway.

"So-so in math, a lick 'n' a promise. Left to her own devices, she'd burn her eyes out reading. Irv, I want to come back to something you said. 'If Alvie is better.' Has the therapy helped?"

"It doesn't look good, Frank," Irv said, shaking his head, revealing his bald spot and brown-gray, thinning hair. "She tires easily. Rests a lot. The worst's been the nausea. She'll go in for an exploratory when we get back to L.A." After a long silence, he lowered his voice, ". . . found tumor."

"*Two more,*" Delia thought she heard him say.

"I'm sure sorry to hear that, Irv," Frank said, laying his hand on his old friend's shoulder.

Every day during their stay, the Meyers-Fishbein guests took turns visiting in one or the other's cottage and entertained themselves by playing bridge. On Saturday morning Delia passed the front window of the appointed cabin Number 9 where the game was being played. She stood tiptoe and peeked in on them, her nose close to the glass. The four players were assembled around a table, their chairs arranged in a square: east, west, north, and south. The men wore Hawaiian shirts with neon-bright, exotic, flowered prints; the ladies sat in long, formless muumuus with bold-colored tropical tones of flamingo pink, violet orchid, canary yellow and orange, and mossy, jungle greens; their feet fitted comfortably in sandals. Delia didn't know who was the older of the two women for they bore a striking resemblance to each other. Both were small in height, freckled in complexion. The sisters had unusually bright, red-colored hair, which made their appearance cheerful, peppery, and snappy. Their fox-colored, red hair reminded Delia of the picture of Cleopatra she had seen on a cigar box in her father's humidor.

They all held cards in their hands in patient, preoccupied study. The men wore their reading glasses. Mr. Meyers wore horned-rimmed, bulky and oversized for his thin, delicately boned face. Mr. Fishbein's spectacles had slipped down over the bridge of his nose making his swarthy face appear idiotic and incompetent.

Mrs. Meyers held Baby in her lap. Then it came her turn to deal. She broke off a soft piece of mint for Baby and passed him over to Mr. Meyers's lap. Unsettled, the dog quivered nervously, his timorous, apprehensive eyes following the flutter of his mistress' slender hands as she shuffled the cards and dealt them out to each player.

"Peek-a-boo, I see you," Mrs. Meyers sang out to Delia when she saw her at the window. "Door's open. Come on in and let us see you, Delia. You can play with Baby. Folks, why don't we leave these cards where they lie, play them out later?"

"All right by me," Trudy Fishbein said.

The other bridge players nodded.

Delia smiled bashfully, standing before them barefooted in the entryway on the cool green linoleum. Mrs. Meyers picked up Baby and delivered her over to the girl's waiting arms.

The dog trembled apprehensively at first, then looked at Delia with his bright, full liquid-brown eyes and nestled himself in her embrace. With the tip of her index finger, she lightly touched one of his large, flaring ears, and he cocked his head at her. He was surely a dog and cute, she thought. But he didn't feel right in her arms. Though his skin was warm and smooth, he lacked long, sleek hair. He was Mrs. Meyers's dog, not hers. Not the dog she wanted.

"Tell me, now," Mrs. Fishbein said, addressing the three adults, "doesn't Delia look more and more like her mother? Cornflower-blue eyes, dark brown hair, slender shoulders."

"She gets prettier every time we see her," Irv Meyers agreed.

Mr. Fishbein, who was short and stocky, grinned in assent. Though he had freshly shaved that morning, his olive complexion already suggested the shadow of a beard.

"We all knew your lovely mother, Delia," Mrs. Meyers said. "Irv introduced your dad to her. Didn't you, sweetheart?"

"True enough. I thought he might be lonely way out here in this little desert town," Irv Meyers said, smiling sheepishly as he briefly removed the owl-like, horned-rimmed glasses that framed his almost effete face. "Good-looking fellow, your dad, plain-spoken, salt-of-the earth. He was my platoon sergeant in the Army. I wasn't a good soldier. Too old, really. If it hadn't been for a young Frank Harper, I don't think I'd have made it."

Delia Harper felt a surge of pride knowing that her father was liked.

"Nettie told me when she first met Frank she thought he was Mexican. She didn't know he was brown from working under the desert sun," Mrs. Meyers said. "You know, Delia, we've been coming to the Green Lantern, oh, long before you were born. All of us, Irv, Trudy, Harvey, me, and your mom and dad used to go across the border to Mexicali, dine on New York cut and salsa and dance to the mariachi at the Mexicali Rosa."

"Dad dance?" Delia Harper said, used to seeing him in his customary workingman's brown khaki.

"And why not?" Mrs. Meyers said. "He especially liked hearing the marimba. You ask him sometime. After your dad had a couple of Carta Blancas, your mother could steer him around the dance floor. Nettie made any partner look good."

Nettie.

The girl felt strange and self-conscious hearing her mother's name spoken aloud. She could imagine her mother dancing, but her father? Never!

As if understanding the girl's discomfort, Baby wiggled and nudged the girl's cheek with his black nose.

The two sisters inclined their red heads toward each other and giggled in unison like school girls.

"He surprised you with his icy-cold nose didn't he?" Trudy Fishbein said.

"I don't know about you Trudy, Harvey," Alvie Meyers said to her sister and brother-in-law, "but I'm bone-weary and ready for a nap. Later on a long, cool shower. I'll see you guys for supper."

"Alvie, we thought we'd ride over to the Salton Sea this afternoon. Mind?" Irv Meyers said.

"Go ahead. Bring me back some of those 'floating rocks.' I can use them in the shop for flower arrangements. Take Delia with you," Alvie Meyers said. "Wouldn't you like to take a swim, Delia? Float? I love floating. When your mother was carrying you, she said, 'My feet are swollen, my belly looks like a watermelon. I want to float in the Salton Sea, belly up, buoyed up like a floating rock, weightless.'"

Belly up. Delia Harper wondered if that was really what her mother would say.

"I don't think your dad will mind," Mrs. Meyers said.

"Did you finish your math problems?" Mr. Meyers said.

The girl nodded.

"All right, then. Go get your bathing suit, a towel. You can walk Baby on the sandy beach. That's just the ticket for him. A place to do his doo-doo. Fresh air. Exercise. Irv, will you bring Baby's leash and a scooper? In the meantime, Baby's staying here 'til you get back. Aren't you, little fellow?" Alvie Meyers said, bending down to kiss Baby. "You're all pluck and heart! Just let me talk to the guy who says you're more mouse than dog," she said to her pet as if rallying him with a pep-talk. "I'll tell him for you, you're no 'wee, sleekit, cowrin, timorous, beastie'!"

"Wait for me, Delia. I'll walk with you to the office, ask your dad's permission," Irv Meyers said.

Then he kissed his wife on the forehead, and on each cheek by turn.

The last evening of their stay, Delia Harper was attracted to Cottage 10, where the Meyers and Fishbeins had dined, by the smell of filet mignon, which had been barbequed on a brazier on the front stoop. Once again she looked in at them in evening attire playing at bridge. Mrs. Fishbein and Mr. Meyers sat opposite each other, his back to the window, his sports jacket folded over an arm of his chair. Mr. Fishbein, too, had laid aside his jacket and faced his partner in white, short-sleeved shirt and bow tie. Mrs. Fishbein, dressed in a lavender dress, sipped something from a glass.

Across from Mr. Fishbein, occupying the chair where she had expected to find Mrs. Meyers, Delia saw the profile of a small, bald-headed stranger. Puzzled, she searched about the room for Mrs. Meyers. Then she saw Baby bobbing his tawny head up from the stranger's lap, and she felt ashamed of herself.

She turned and looked away, startled by what she had seen: Mrs. Meyers, her naked head a chalky white without her red, red hair!

Frightened and alarmed, Delia Harper rushed back home to her own cottage.

Frank Harper brushed his newspaper aside, as soon as he caught sight of his daughter's scared, flushed face. "Here, here now. What's made you upset?" he said, catching her up, enfolding his brown arms around her, and setting her on his lap.

"Mrs. Meyers," she said, trying to catch her breath.

"Just take it easy. What about Mrs. Meyers?"

"Mrs. Meyers doesn't have any hair."

"Ah, so you saw her without a wig? Its been heating up. Too hot for wearing one."

His daughter put her chin down, avoiding his gray eyes. "I thought she had real hair. I didn't know."

"No, of course you didn't. You were shocked. Now then, Alvie's the same Mrs. Meyers that we like. She has developed some bad tumors. Her doctor's using radiation to destroy them. She's shouldering treatment very well. She and Irv both are. We want to remember to keep them in our prayers. Let me try putting this in ways I'm familiar. You know how we've stopped along the roadside to look at the alfalfa growing in our valley?"

The girl nodded.

"I've grown fields of alfalfa in my day. Well, let the healthy field stand for Alvie Meyers's body. Okay? Sometimes locoweed gets in with the healthy green lucerne, wants to spread. Like tumors. Then I'd have to burn out patches, kill the bad locoweed. And I'd have to kill off some of the healthy alfalfa to get to the root of the trouble. Something like Alvie Meyers's hair. Make sense?"

"A little bit," Delia Harper said. "Will it grow back?"

"As far as I know. What else's on your mind?" he asked, grinning broadly at her.

She hesitated, desiring once again to tell him of her pet fancy. And yet, lest she try his patience, she held back. Instead, she asked, "What's a 'marimba'?"

"Where'd you hear of mirambas?"

"Mrs. Meyers said you liked them."

"Remember the toy xylophone you had when you were

little? Maybe you don't. You were just a tot. Anyway, it's somewhat like a bigger xylophone. I like the cheerful sound a marimba makes. Like rhythmic chimes."

"I remember," she said, wanting hard to remember.

Hunter

Cabin Number 1 of Frank Harper's Green Lantern Motel smelled of the after-breakfast aromas of fried bacon and eggs and smoky-tasting coffee. The sound of a bulletin being read from the California Farm Labor Bureau droned from a radio placed on top of the refrigerator. Delia Harper put aside her book, *Lad, of Sunnybank,* and watched her father prepare the lunch she would take with her to her fourth-grade class at Acacia County School five miles from El Centro. His dark face, browned from the sun, was intent and purposeful at a perfunctory task. With a steel-bladed butcher knife, he carved cold beef from the Diamond Jim pot roast he customarily simmered on Sundays with fresh tomatoes, green Anaheim chili peppers, yellow onions, cloves of garlic, and red beans.

He placed an ample wedge of sliced meat between two thick slices of bakery bread. "Want horseradish?"

Delia turned up her nose, shaking her head vigorously. Her dark, brown hair, which her father had plaited into one thick braid, swung behind her neck down to her waist.

"Okay for you. More for me," he said good-naturedly.

"Tell me again about Uncle Les' work horses."

"Not about his twenty-six milking cows? Named alphabetically, Alice through Zelda."

"Horses."

Her father wrapped the sandwich in paper and slipped it into a brown paper sack along with an apple.

"Let's see. Well, you have to keep an eye on them. They act like big, lazy overgrown kids sometimes," he said, remembering the coltish-acting, great-rumped Clydesdales he had worked with as a boy on his uncle's dairy farm in Idaho. "Especially when you first harness them up after they've been quartered in a barn most of the winter."

"Why won't you let me have a horse?"

He shook his head in mock exasperation, having heard her plea many times, lifted a boiling kettle of water from the stove, and doused hot, scalding liquid over the kitchen sink counters. Then he scrubbed them down with a bristle brush. "Now, Delia. We've been all through this." He reached into an upper cupboard for the bottle of cheap, Mexican tequila he used as a disinfectant and poured some of it out on the counter, continuing to scour. "Where would you ride? We don't own a ranch. We have the Green Lantern Motel, right off Interstate 8." He picked up a coffee cup, and, discovering a chip on its rim, pitched it into a garbage can.

"Did Uncle Les and Aunt Rilma have a dog?"

"Never. Not in the farmhouse. Never in the barn around fresh milk."

"But if I can't have a horse, why won't you let me have a dog? I'd shower and scrub him down everyday. Mr. Terhune's Lad doesn't have fleas."

"I don't give a damn about Mr. Terhune. Dogs are filthy. I've told you time and time again. They carry disease."

He set his jaw hard and took down from a wall hook an old, weather-beaten Panama hat his wife had bought for him on their honeymoon weekend in Santa Catalina. He pushed the hat down on his head and strode toward the front door of the cabin, preparing to leave for his registry office, adjacent to the motel units.

"Now, don't dawdle, Delia. You don't want to miss the school bus."

Delia sighed and, following her father out the door, walked slowly in the direction of the bus stop. She didn't understand her father's wrath and meanness toward dogs. She pitied any lost, wayward dog, without master and home, that foraged its way down the edge of the highway until he wandered onto the graveled court of the Green Lantern, there to amble toward her father's registry office. If her father spied the wretch, he raced outside and grabbed up a few stones from the pile by the door and hurled them one at a time at the accursed brute until the vanquished pariah fled from the inhospitable motel keeper with its tail between its legs and vanished out of sight.

Her spirits brightened when she caught sight of her playmate, Hollis Crow, waving to her impatiently from the stop, and she ran to catch up to him.

They stood together on the side of the highway, not far from the entrance into the courtyard of Harper's Green Lantern Modern Motel, where a sign read either Vacancy or No Vacancy, depending on the circumstances, and, underneath in smaller black letters, No Dogs.

Cars swished past them on their way to town. Two expensive yellow Caterpillar tractors rolled by toward the rich green alfalfa fields and sugarbeet crops under cultivation. The morning air carried aloft two distinct sweetnesses; one a rank distillation, heady, spoiled, a cloying odor like boiling brown syrup exuded by beet pulp from a sugar refinery five miles away in El Centro; the other a natural honey-like freshness of green clover, which drifted to their nostrils from acres and acres of uncut lucerne in nearby pastures.

The bus stop was near a portion of the remains of an old road which had buckled during an earthquake. A new highway had replaced the old one. The vertical fault line made the ground lying parallel to the new road uneven and bumpy, and a collapsed depression in the earth had created a jagged-shaped, shallow burrow, running approximately six feet in length, its depth varying from one to two feet.

Delia and Hollis grumbled about how the school bus broke down and was habitually slow and late. Hollis was a reluctant schoolboy. He made no attempt to conceal a pack of Lucky Strikes, whose red bull's-eye logo glared out with conspicuous defiance from a pocket of his worn bib overalls. He would have liked an excuse not to have to attend school that day, so he could go hunting for rabbits in the desert brush with his newly acquired .22 Marlin bolt-action rifle.

"It has a clip magazine that holds eight shells. I can wing anything that moves," he said. "It's as easy as a water pistol. Only you shoot bullets. That's what. You plink away at jackrabbits or doves and wing anything that moves. Like that magpie over yonder." He lifted an imaginary rifle to his shoulder, squinted an eye, and feigned taking aim at the black-and-white-feathered bird, which chattered down at them and heckled from the branch of a mesquite. It seemed to mock the boy's silly play by flitting from higher bough to higher bough, a flicker of black feathers, a flutter of white, the streak of an impudent, black tail. At the pinnacle of the tree, the magpie shrieked, wildly leapt in the air and flapped its wings and lit and pecked at some locust pods with his sharp, curved beak until they shook loose and popped on the ground almost near the children's feet.

"I'll get you, Hollis," Delia cried, rushing in front of the boy and standing in his line of fire. "He's just an old bird. Just a dumb bird."

"Okay. Okay," he said, and shoved her out of his way just as the magpie took flight.

He was in a sulk, and she moved away from him quickly. By a trick of thought, Delia associated the colors of the magpie's feathers with the distorted, old-fashioned black and white woodcut engravings in her worn copy of *Grimms' Fairy Tales*. She was especially drawn to the illustrations even though, whenever she opened up the book to them, she feared what she would see. If she turned the pages to one place, the book would have its own way and fall open to a print depicting a dark country churchyard where a sexton, having hidden himself away in a coffin, lay fast asleep. If she found herself at another part of the book, she might come to a printed scene of a dark forest and the humped shape of the witch, who imprisoned children. The picture showed the witch poking at Hansel's stomach with her gnarled, bony finger as she waited impatiently for the boy to fatten up, so she could kill him and roast him and gobble him up like succulent suckling pig. Several pages ahead of this print led her to a picture of Snow White and Rose Red. She could behold the two sisters as they discovered an ancient, withered dwarf with a white beard flowing to the ground at his feet. But most dreadful of all the woodcuts she might turn to was the sight of a princess, high up in a room in a castle battlement, who looks down from one of twelve windows in the tower and views at its bottom ninety-seven decapitated suitors, whose hideous heads, wide-eyed and gaped-mouthed, have been impaled upon stakes. These frightening scenes left an indelible impression on Delia and transformed themselves in her dreams. If she were in half slumber on a dark, gray morning and heard the anxious cries of cranes flying from distant rice marshlands to the Green Lantern and over its rooftops, their whoops sounded to her like the wild gibberish of black-winged witches in flight.

Her daydreaming was interrupted when a flat-bed truck, conveying a crowded load of Mexican field workers, approached the two children at the bus stop. Before the vehicle lurched onward toward a distant field of sugar beets, some of the dark-skinned men wearing broad straw hats and white shirts smiled and waved their arms in greeting to them. Their friendly distraction caused Delia to reopen a conversation with Hollis about his favorite object.

"Hollis?"

"What?"

"Can your .22 kill a witch?"

"Whadda ya mean a witch?"

"Flying witches."

"Oh, like ghosts? I dunno. Let me think on it."

She looked at Hollis' glistening black, cropped hair. He was unlike the other migrant children, who were usually ubiquitously blue-eyed, tow-headed blonds. He was tall for his age, hard and sinewy of frame. He had told Delia that his ancestors were Plains Indians, great warriors and horsemen. Except for her small stature, she resembled Hollis enough to have been mistaken for his sister. Like her, he was also in the fourth grade although he was two years older than she. The Crow family, his father, stepmother, aunt and uncle, and sister, Corliss, who was thirteen and already married to a packing foreman by the name of Ben Honeybee, came to the Imperial Valley season and worked in farm labor or at local canneries on the outskirts of town. They rented two cabins from Delia's father from winter to early spring before migrating to the San Joaquin Valley to harvest grapes.

All of a sudden, as Delia and Hollis stood on the wayside of the highway, expecting to see the school bus at any moment, a rangy stray, a reddish mahogany and black collie-shepherd crossbreed appeared seemingly from out of nowhere and gamboled up to them, wagging his long, bushy tail. Delia backed away timidly from the strange wolfy dog while he bowed his head and forepaws and fawned before them. Then he raised his dainty head and opened up his jaws and arched his upper lip in a roguish, collie-like smile.

"Do you think he's rabid?" Delia said.

"Don't be stupid." Hollis said. "Can't you see he's a smiling dog?"

He hunched down by the dog's side and petted his heavy, dark coat. "I wonder where he comes from? He don't have a collar, no nuthin'. He's pretty young, too. Still has puppy smell. Milky-like."

The mongrel frisked in and out between them. With his wet, black nose he sniffed down their legs, right to each child's pair of leather shoes. First he smelled Delia's high-polished Oxfords, the ones her father kept shined and had purchased for her in the nearby Mexican border town of Mexicali. Next he nosed Hollis' scuffed, hand-me-down workboots, one size too large. Like manacles about his ankles, they caused the boy to shamble. The dog pranced from one child to the other, as if in high glee, and nudged each one's brown paper lunch sack, his pink tongue glistening with saliva, panting in playful camaraderie.

Delia supposed that as usual Hollis carried in his lunch two sticky, clumsily made sandwiches of Skippy peanut butter and grape jelly on white Langendorf bread. Delia tired of having a meat sandwich for lunch. It didn't take Hollis too long to figure out that he could finagle out of her one of hers for one of his. He called the swap "an even Indian trade."

The male shepherd-mix nosed winsomely at Delia's sack until she reached into it and fished out half a roast beef sandwich, which she threw out on the ground The stray wolfed the portion down and groveled before her for more, cocking an ear, barking, and finally training his deep-set eyes on her.

"Hey, there, you beggar," Hollis said. "Gimme that." He grabbed Delia's sack away from her and raised both of their bags high up over his head out of reach of the dog.

The mongrel's keen nose traced the pungent scents of flesh and oil, sugar and salt emitting from the lunches. He leapt up on his hindlegs and placed his forepaws across Hollis' chest and the upper top of the boy's bib overalls. Then he stretched his long, shaggy neck and smooth white and black muzzle and licked Hollis' mouth and face. The boy smiled and revealed a hiding dimple in each cheek.

"You can be my hunter," he said.

Delia wished they could ditch school and coax the dog to follow them back to the Green Lantern, where they could look for a place to hide him away from her father's knowledge and keep the dog as their secret pet forever. He could hunt with Hollis all day, and, when night fell, she could sneak "Hunter" into her bedroom in the cabin after her father was asleep. He could sleep at the foot of her bed and guard her from the wiles of the old, haggy witch who came invisibly in the night and poked her crooked nose into the ears of sleeping children and gave them howling earaches or spat infectious juice into their slumberous eyes and made their eyelashes stick together, yellow-scabbed and itchy. Just a husky growl from Hunter's throat would chase away the hag who whorled through the tiny mesh of the window screen in many disguises. She was the buzzing, pesky mosquito who brought chills and fever. She could make the bed feel as if it spun about the room in vertigo circles. She was the chigger picked up unknowingly in the high, dry foxtails that clung to socks and wheedled its way up to a soft, resting stomach and burrowed into the navel and left a nasty, swollen welt. If Delia had a nightmare, she could cry out "Hunter," and he would crawl up from the foot of the blanket and reach her, his hairy nape nuzzling close to her face.

"Let's call him 'Hunter'," Delia was ready to say aloud, when almost in spite of her thought, the dog answered to an instinctive, erratic impulse and turned his attention away from the children to hunt a brown jackrabbit bounding across the open highway toward a field beyond them.

The reddish-brown and black dog Delia had fallen in love with plunged headlong after the hare into the on-coming flow of morning traffic.

At first, Delia and Hollis watched in dumb horror when the stray dog was struck sideways by a passing motorist. But then Hollis acted nimbly. He reached down and loosened the laces of his oversized boots. Once free of them, he loped lithe of foot after the wounded pup.

Yelping piteously, the stricken dog hobbled in blind panic toward the other side of the road as motorists swerved to avoid hitting him and the barefooted boy who raced after him in pursuit.

The school bus arrived shortly after the accident occurred and creaked to a stop just as Delia saw the wolfy dog she wanted to call Hunter limp to the side of the highway and fall down in a huddle near the burrow on the vertical fault line.

She had lost sight of Hollis.

In her hands she held two lunch sacks though she couldn't remember exactly when she had gained possession of them.

"Hurry up. Hurry up," the bus driver yelled. "I'm already late. Make up your mind if you're gettin' in. Say, I'm supposed to pick up two kids here. Where's the Mexican?"

Delia knew he meant Hollis, but she shrugged her shoulders.

She hesitated before pulling herself up to board, feeling wretched and guilty about leaving the scene of the accident and yet fearing the consequences if she hung back and did not go on to school.

Before boarding, she placed her lunch bag on the ground next to the worn boots Hollis had abandoned and flung by the wayside in his haste to pursue the wounded dog. Then she took a deep breath and entered the open door of the crowded bus with its load of active, yelling children who looked forward to the end of the week and the beginning of summer vacation. Only when she had reached the back of the bus and found an empty seat on the hump did she cry in silence as she looked out a window toward the scene of the accident, her face heated and forlorn and desolate.

At last she caught a brief glimpse of Hollis. He stood over the earthquake burrow, seeming small in the distance as the bus heaved onward past fields of sugar beets and brown, zigzagged shapes of field workers bent over in labor.

At the close of the school day, in the long-shadowed afternoon, the bus returned her and the other children to their home stops. As Delia walked away from the departing bus toward the motel, she almost passed by without noticing the shallow earthquake crack resembling a burrow, which ran near the shoulder of the highway. Her father had explained to her that many years before her birth, the Imperial Valley had undergone a severe tremor of enormous magnitude. The crack in the earth was the result of this natural phenomenon. Somehow, she felt peculiarly drawn to the mysterious oddity and stopped at one end of it and peered down. There, at the bottom of the trench, lying in a coagulated, rusty-brown pool of dried blood, surrounded by a thick, black cloud of flies jealously veiling him, sprawled the carcass of a dog—the mongrel yearling she had wanted to claim as her own and had fed a portion of her beef sandwich.

Her father had told her that hurt creatures often instinctively crawl away by themselves and hide, then, with time, either heal or die. She reasoned that this was why the injured dog fled in its pain and disappeared into the den-like burrow.

She looked down once more at the sight of the rigid dog, and then drew back from the crack in the earth in repulsion and pity. He had lost his milky puppy-smell and, with the heat of the intense desert sun, there rose from his corpse the smell of putrification. Like the flies, ants, too, had sniffed out the carcass and had begun their ravagement. They had set the rich black and red mahogany coat rippling alive with their steady, crawling battalions. She puckered up her nose and mouth in disgust and turned her back on the hole and ran away from it in fear.

In the last week of June, Hollis Crow left the Imperial Valley with his itinerant family to pick grapes in the vineyards near Fresno. After the Crows left and their cabin lay vacant, Delia picked some scarlet and while oleander blossoms from the bushes that grew in front of it and took them to the earthquake crack, the gravesite of the mongrel dog. On this return visit, she observed, with morbid fascination, mysterious disturbances on his body. His reddish brown and black fur had thinned away; there appeared two open sockets in his skull, where once had glowed luminous brown eyes. Centered in the bone of his forehead was a third round hole, the size of a shirt button, where a .22 bullet had entered. Though the jawbone remained long and wolf-like, the canine fangs sharp and menacing, parts of the spinal skeleton were absent; segments of the vertebrae had disappeared. Under the fiery sun, its dog-ness had flattened, sunk, receded farther and farther away into elemental dissolution, the internment resolved into the salty, alkaline sod.

The Turtle

"Never go to the percolation pond alone," Frank Harper warned Delia, his nine-year-old daughter. "I knew of a little boy who drowned in a pond like the one way out there." Frank Harper pointed in the direction behind the Green Lantern Motel, their home and his place of business for the past ten years.

Where was his mother? How did they get him out? the girl wondered. But she only asked, "Was he really dead?"

"As dead as the skunk we saw spread out on Highway 8. Remember what I'm telling you for your own good." As he spoke, he nudged the sleeve of her blue school dress and reappraised the work of his hands. As usual, before she had left for the school bus that morning, he had parted her hair straight down the middle and plaited two long, brown braids. By now, late in the afternoon, they had become undone, and he saw that she had lost one of the red rubber bands, though he made no mention of it.

He tipped his chin slightly to his right and then to the left to acknowledge the cultivated fields of lucerne that grew to the edge of the desert highway on both sides of the motel.

"Stay way from the pond and the irrigation ditches. They open the floodgates and run the water to the crops." Since his wife had left them five years before, and he had to keep an eye on Delia by himself, he always feared for the worst.

They could hear the fields of alfalfa sigh and rustle, and smell the air full of sleepy pollen and earth scents.

"I'll remember," she said, fidgeting and averting her brown eyes from his stern gaze. Close by her bare feet, on the harsh, warm gravel stones of the Green Lantern's courtyard, a gravelly tan, white-splotched horned toad had squatted momentarily and caught her attention. Extending one foot out toward it very slowly, balancing herself as though waiting her turn at hopscotch, she tried to bump her big toe against his flat, spiney body before he hopped away out of her reach.

She thought of how moist and cool and oozingly muddy to the toes the banks of the irrigation ditches felt. She had never gone into a canal all by herself, having been partly heedful of her father's warning of the danger of drowning, of being caught in the muddy currents and being swept away by the gurgling rush of water if the floodgates were to open. She had played along the banks of the irrigation ditches with migrant workers' children, whose parents came to work seasonally as farm laborers in California's Imperial Valley and sometimes rented cabins for a short duration at her father's Green Lantern Motel. A few times, under the heat of the furious sun, she had disobeyed her father and had gone into an irrigation canal with playmates she had made at the autocourt. She had slid down a muddy embankment with them into a ditch of shallow, refreshing water, wading side by side up to the waist, splashing and giggling, slippery-wet. As they played in the cooling water, they talked sometimes of going to the percolation pond and looking for an ancient turtle rumored to be living at the bottom.

"Is there one really?" she asked her father more than once.

"Yes," he assured her. "I've sighted him a time or two. Sometimes he'll sun himself on the bank. Mostly, he hides away. He's wily. 'Gramps' had to be wily to get to a ripe, old age. He's gigantic, I'd say." He spread his hands in the air, far apart. "Say, two feet in length. Maybe he's a hundred years. Maybe more."

He bent down to her and peered hard into her face, dark-complexioned as was his own, speaking to her as if he could read her thoughts.

"Listen close. Don't go out there by yourself. The water level goes up and down. Sometimes up over six feet. Haven't I told you about the Jacksons' kid? Drowned. Wait for me. I'll take you with me next time I plumb. 'Gramps' might show up."

Springtime was Frank Harper's busiest time running the motel. He was preoccupied with making repairs on the cabin units and renting them out.

"When are we going to the pond?" she asked him now and again.

"I've got my hands plenty full now, Delia. I said we'd go sometime. Don't pester me. Sometime is sometime."

Her face fell, and she turned away from him in disappointment.

When school recessed at the end of April and the daylight hours lengthened toward summer, the girl's curiosity about seeing the turtle got the best of her. One summery day, she wandered farther and farther away from the grounds of the motel, heedless of her father's admonition.

She came to a hand-painted "No Trespassing" sign, which she recognized as being in her father's hand printing, and stopped short before it, lingering long enough to read the black lettering, sounding out the syllables slowly, conscious momentarily of its warning message. For perhaps a moment or two, a small, still voice of fear rose up inside her as she remembered the little drowned boy. Then she looked about her. She saw only dry tumbleweeds, circular, prickled, and at rest.

Her overwhelming desire to see the turtle subdued her anxiety, and she boldly turned her back on the sign, padding past it on rapid bare feet.

There, suddenly before her, lay the pond, placid, flat, motionless. Not even a slight desert breeze stirred the branches of the dwarfed cottonwood trees surrounding it.

She lay down near the pond and leaned over the moist bank, the warmth of the afternoon sun on her bare head and shoulders. She saw the outline of her face and the thin straps of her yellow sundress in the wavy reflection of the pool. Tiny schools of slender black minnows and bulbous-headed polly-wogs whipped back and forth in the water, and she wished she had thought of bringing an empty coffee can with her to use for scooping some of them up. Water mosquitos skittered by. She strained her eyes, trying to accustom them to the water's shadowy darkness. She stretched her body farther out over the surface, peering down and squinting until she thought she glimpsed four greenish legs paddling rhythmi-cally in slow motion down to the murky bottom. She became so excited she held her breath and dared not breathe as she watched in awe the hump of an enormous black and brown checkered shell, a head protruding forward from it, and claws drawing back and forth from the body in drowsy ani-mation.

All of a sudden, just at the moment when a heady dizziness overcame her, she felt a strong tug on her shoulders, pulling her away from the pond.

She was in the grasp of her father's hands.

Her father did not switch her legs with thin willow branches as he had done when she was a littler girl and disobeyed him. But he was not without an ingenious punishment that seemed to have occurred to him from an arbitrary inspiration.

For many years, before Frank Harper had joined the army, even before he had married Delia's mother, he had saved all kinds of construction nails, much as a man might collect postage stamps or various denominations of coins. In time, he had acquired a huge assortment of bright, ordinary nails suitable for use in general carpentry as well as an extraordinary supply of special types of nails for specific jobs like casing or scaffolding or roofing or cabinet-making, in which he took great pleasure. For this long period of time, in the quick convenience of a moment, he had pitched the odd one he bought or found or had no immediate use for into a deep wooden barrel, thinking that one day he would find the time to sort them all out by type and place them properly by kind and value in separate bins. But, over the years, the mixture of nails went unsorted and accumulated in the drum, growing exceedingly in mass, weight, and bulky proportion.

As her punishment, for a long half-day—from eight o'clock in the morning until noontime—Delia's father set her to the task of sorting out various-sized nails that he had thrown indifferently into the cavernous mouth of the great wooden drum standing in his storage workshop, a small room located just behind the wall of the motel's registry office.

"I'm at my wit's end with you. You're going to be where I know where you are. I won't have you galavantin' about as you please. Like a wild Indian." Then Frank Harper shoved the weight of his muscular body against the heavy barrel and unleashed a torrent of nails, thousands of them; some showered down into a huge metal pile, while others spilled out and rolled willy-nilly over the cold, concrete floor.

He wheeled a portable metal table over to Delia, who sat on a stool her father had built for her seventh birthday. Opening out a deep drawer in the table, he pulled out a number of stacked metal trays and laid them out on the floor beside her. "Watch close, now. I'll show you how to sort them."

He picked out a few nails of the same size from the huge mound and handed one of them to Delia. It felt cold and smooth and lifeless, flat on one end, pointed and sharp on the other. It warmed in the contact of her small palm.

"In the olden days a smithy hand-forged the nails," her father explained. "You paid two pennies a hundred for small nails like the one incher you've got."

Delia looked down at the gray, silvery nail and nodded. It was a senseless object to her. Its solid, meaningless form made her feel empty and disconnected. How she ached for the freedom she knew in the sunshine, outside the barren, metallic, faintly nutmeg-smelling storage room.

"Nowadays 'penny' means length. A box of these is marked '2D' for length. I use these a lot. Drop these in one of the metal drawers," he said. When the nails he plunked into the drawer landed, the metal tinkled merrily in the dreary room.

"Let's see if I can locate some four-penny nails," he said, working his hands over the heap of nails until he had made a find.

He gave her one, and she clutched it gingerly.

"Don't be afraid of it. It won't bite you," he said, forgetting for the moment his role as taskmaster, speaking playfully in the friendly, good-humored tone he used when he played poker with her and patiently explained to her, more than once, the value of the suits in ascending order, lowest hand to highest, giving in genially to her whim that they keep all the jokers in the game and also call the deuces wild.

Then he remembered himself and resumed his matter-of-factness, pointing out to her a nail "exactly two-and-a-half inches."

He showed her how he wanted her to separate the large twenty-penny nails from thirty-penny nails, forty-penny nails from fifty-penny nails, sixty-penny nails, all appropriate to each kind.

"I'll be working on accounts in the office next door. If you want to go to the bathroom or anything, pound hard on the front wall. Otherwise, you are to stay put where I know where you are. I want you to think twice before you go runnin' off just as you damn well please." He would return at noon with her lunch. She could eat "on the job site."

Her eyes smarted in frustration. As soon as he turned his back on her and reached for the doorknob, she muttered low enough for him not to hear, "I hate you. You're old and mean. Mean and old."

She angrily picked up loose nails from the floor and hurled them at a bare wall. The steel clanked and clattered and rattled onto the concrete floor in dissonant jangles. Then the chill room fell silent, and she was alone downcast in her Herculean task.

At first, as she sorted out the nails from the great stack of gleaming metal and pitched them into their appropriate beds, they made clinking sounds or landed with dull thuds.

After the minutes passed into an hour and she had sorted out iron pins with rounded heads that resembled capitol T's, a heavy, monotonous refrain thumped around and around in her brain: *T for turtle, T for turtle, T for turtle*. If she selected a thin, headless nail, the relentless monotone ceased until she again selected a round, T-headed one. Then the incessant rhythm resumed.

Sharp nails, pins, needles, nettles, the rusty dust on her fingers and palms reminded her without relief of the miller's beautiful daughter, closed away in a dismal room, set at a wheel and spindle, commanded to spin straw into gold, the king threatening to put her to death should she fail. Now she began to understand the weight of the miller's daughter's task, her frustration over forever spinning straw into gold, the meaning of anguish behind the words in the fairy tale, "She sighed with a heavy heart." She heard the bright cries of children playing and shouting to each other outside while she toiled in detention in a sunless, drab room.

At least I saw him, she consoled herself defiantly. I really did find the turtle. He lives in the pond forever and ever.

Delia's chest tightened into a hard knot. A dead, gray metallic taste had formed in her mouth and dribbled down the back of her throat. She imagined it drying to yellow dust in the pit of her stomach.

Her fingers cramped and stiffened. The nails pricked her, and she earned a sore rawness for her pains. She felt a burning sensation on the palms of her hands, and she cried bitterly. Then she lost sensation in the tips of her fingers. She tightened her hands into fists and clenched and unclenched them to revive their blood and warmth.

At last, just as she listlessly dropped another dull nail into a metal tray, her father entered the storage room.

He looked about him and saw the many different nails Delia had sorted in particular trays.

"Why I am surprised," he said. "You've done a yeoman job."

When he looked down at her hands, swollen, red and scratched, he set his jaw hard in self-reproach and contrition.

"I did not mean for you to be hurt. Let's go into the office, and I'll find some ointment for your fingers and sore thumbs."

"Do I have to do more nails?"

"No. You've done good. I'll come back and sweep them up off the floor."

Jersey Joe Versus the Rock

Frank Harper took his daughter's hand, and they entered "Happy's" from the rear door. The long narrow barroom smelled of rancid beer and smoke, dank perspiration, and urine from the toilets.

Happy stood behind the double bar, a dead stogy in his mouth. When he saw Harper and Delia enter through the back door, he removed the cigar and waved the stub in greeting to them. He smiled a broad, toothless grin at Delia. No one was playing pool. Most of Happy's customers were idling, drinking at the bar, sitting on the barstools.

Frank Harper looked forward to the championship boxing match, scheduled to be televised live from Madison Square Garden, between Jersey Joe Walcott, defending his heavyweight title, and Rocky Marciano. Having only a small television at the Green Lantern Motel, he took his nine-year-old daughter, Delia, with him into town so he could view the fight on the large television at a public bar.

On the Saturday afternoon of the exhibition fight, Frank Harper had driven them in his old green Chevy down the Imperial Desert Highway to El Centro. He parked his car in an alley behind H.A. Happy Davis' Pool and Lo-Ball Parlor in a weathered neighborhood of dilapidated clapboard houses, saloons, a second-hand furniture surplus store, and a pawnbroker's shop at the end of State Street on the outskirts of town.

Two or three of the men at the bar turned around in their seats and called out to the newcomers as they came in the back door.

"Hey, Frank, what's doin'? That your daughter? Sure cute."

"She's a dandy," the father said, his face animated.

"Ain't this gonna be a hell of a fight?" another man said.

"Don't pay attention to their talk, Delia. I don't talk rough around you. I never did around your mother, neither," the father said, motioning with his chin toward the men lined up at the bar. "Can't be helped," he said, shaking his head. "I'll bet they don't talk rough at home."

Though the television was set up at the rear end of the bar, where most of the men had already gathered, Frank Harper led his daughter to the front, near the State Street entrance to the saloon. The door opened wide to the street and let in fresh air and bits of slanting light from the afternoon sun.

Father and daughter walked the full length of the long, box-shaped poolhall toward three unoccupied barstools. After they reached the end of the counter, Frank Harper stooped down to give Delia a lift up to the last stool.

"Don't set her there, Frank," Happy called from the far side of the bar. "Stool's busted."

They saw that the stool tipped slightly to one side and the red, vinyl-coated seat cover was ripped.

The father then helped Delia onto the second empty stool and waited behind her until she had adjusted herself to the height and her long, skinny legs dangled down. Afterwards he slid into the seat alongside of her.

"Do you want to try a bowl of Happy's chili? I'm told it

gives you character and grows hair on your chest," he said, grinning.

Delia made a face and squinched up her nose. "Can't I have a hamburger with French fries 'n' mustard and ketchup?"

"Happy can you fix us up a couple of burgers," Frank Harper called to the bartender.

"Match'll be on pretty soon. How's about hot dogs," Happy returned.

"Okay, Hap. Bring a couple of dogs." Then he ordered their drinks.

Happy came down to them with two hot dogs on buns. Then he made a return trip, carrying their drinks. He set a tall, icy glass of ginger ale with a maraschino cherry on it before the girl and a stein of draught ABC beer in front of the father.

Frank reached for a salt shaker and shook it over the foamy head of beer.

"Dad, does the salt make the beer taste better?"

"It's good for a change. Like on a hot day. Wanna taste?"

"Bitter," she said, taking a sip.

There was a buzz of anticipation among the row of men, some seated, some standing. Then the walls of the dense, boxy poolhall shook with the brazen hoops and shouts of fans as the television screen showed the boxers entering the ring, Jersey Joe Walcott in white trunks, the Rock in black trunks.

The deafening din from the colossal crowd in Madison Square Garden and the ear-splitting clamor of the fans in Happy's created a strange, redoubling effect, the reality of noise in a close saloon and the reverberation of sounds from a coliseum juxtaposed, paradoxically blended, but separated in narrow space.

There before her on the screen over the bar were two

brawny, muscular men, one as black as patent leather, the other tall and light-skinned. One wore dark trunks, the other white trunks, and each had great, oversized gloves and boxing shoes.

"My bet's on Jersey Joe, the favorite," Frank said, pointing out for Delia the boxer wearing white trunks.

The boxers feinted punches, then traded punches. Delia watched them at blows with each other in measured bravura, their bodies sweaty.

"Foul! Foul," she heard, and the referee came between the boxers, locked in a clinch, and separated them.

A bell rang. "End of the first round," Frank told Delia. "We're going for fifteen."

Delia lost interest in the match and toyed with the candied maraschino cherry. It appeared magnified to twice its size in the glass. She pulled it out of the ginger ale by its stem, and it shrank in size. Then she returned it to the soda and dallied with it. Once more it appeared huge. She pulled it out again and bit into it. The maraschino cherry, with its rubbery, pickled texture looked better than it tasted.

She had never tasted a fresh cherry. When her mother had lived with them, she had sometimes bought two cans of Queen Anne cherries, pinkish and yellow colored, and made a pie. She cut out slices from it, still warm from the oven, and served up each piece with fresh whipped cream. Her mother let her lick the thickened, sweet cream, flavored with vanilla, which clung to the blades of the eggbeater.

A neon ABC beer sign hung over the bar, and the glaring light blinked on and off. When it lit up, it cast a reddish-orange reflection on her father's profile as he watched the progress of the prize fight. His hair was as dark and as straight as her own. She did not possess curly auburn-colored hair like her mother. But, like her mother, she had hundreds of freckles on her face and arms. When she was a very little girl, she'd sit on her father's lap and ask him to paint every freckle on her arms with bright iodine.

"What are you up to?" he said.

"War paint," she said.

"Savvy. Pick out twelve."

"On each arm," she insisted.

"All right. Even-Steven," he agreed.

Her father's face was the color of browned summer berries from day labor under the desert sun. He was muscular. She'd make him smile in amusement when she asked him to flex his forearms, so she could feel how hard his biceps were. He would have been considered handsome in an austere sort of way, but he was hard of hearing and scowled often from straining to hear what someone had to say. He was always telling Delia to speak up.

Under the roars from the television and the noisiness in the bar, Delia heard piping squeaks that seemed to be coming from the seat next to her. She poked a finger into the springs of the broken bar stool and touched warm, wiggling flesh. She pulled on the matting, opening it up wider, and saw three pink, hairless squirmers—tiny blind mice with open mouths, squeaking hungrily, all of a nest.

She remembered the nursery round:

"Three blind mice, three blind mice,
See how they run, See how they run
They all ran after the farmer's wife . . . "

Delia nudged her father.

He looked over to her and then down where she pointed.

"Don't monkey with them. They're nasty. Might be rabid," he said. "Here, take my seat. I'll stand."

Delia moved into her father's seat, and Frank stood behind her.

Suddenly a babel of noise erupted from the crowd at Madison Square Garden. The shouters in Happy's whooped and hollered. Marciano slumped on the ropes, faltered, then came forward as if in a stupor. The crowd cheered him on.

Then Walcott knocked the Rock to the ground. He lay prone on the mat—"One, two, three," went the count.

"Get up, Rocky! Get up, Rock!" fans chanted.

Happy's was in an uproar.

Eyes closed, Rocky made it up from the mat, back on his feet.

Shouters jostled each other, pounding their fists on the bar. Some jabbed each other in the ribs, shouting and stamping their feet.

"Come on Rocky! Come on Rocky!" they screamed at the top of their lungs.

Blood poured from Marciano's nose. His body was covered with blood, bruises, lather.

Delia grimaced and slipped down from her seat.

Marciano came after Jersey Joe, pummel after pummel, blow after blow to the head, to his upper body, deep down to the gut. Then the Rock laid Walcott out. KO'ed him in the thirteenth round.

"That's that. Too bad, too bad," Frank said, his jaw set hard. Then he went to Delia's side. She stood before the broken bar stool.

"Where's their mother?" she said.

"I don't know. C'mon along now," he said, taking her hand.

She looked in, for one last time, on the mice buried in their nest, suckling the air with open mouths.

Posing

"Clive Adams is my favorite author," a buoyant voice said to a woman gazing at a pen-and-ink sketch of the writer. She turned from the picture to glance at a short, middle-aged stranger. She had seen few visitors in the De Young Memorial Museum this midweek afternoon, and, up until this moment, she'd had the exhibition room of Larry Theobald's portrait drawings virtually to herself. She saw that the man's sandy-brown hair was receding, and his coffee-colored jacket had a red AIDS ribbon attached to its lapel.

"My very favorite," he said again, smiling and claiming her attention, standing next to her at the same height.

"I haven't found the patience to read his works on Eastern mysticism, but I've enjoyed his personal travel memoirs," she said, noting that the man's maroon tie was knotted nattily and set off with a gold tie tack. "*Interlaken Express* especially." The book brought her a pleasant memory. She'd had a copy of it on her desk when she had been doing a research project years ago for the American Embassy in Bern, where she had met her husband.

"Especially *Interlaken*," he said, warming to a kindred sympathy. "Ever been?"

"To the Alps?" She nodded. "I've been many times. Beautiful. In fact, I lived there for awhile."

"Lucky you! Me? Not yet. But someday."

She had let her long dark hair return to its natural color earlier that autumn, and swept it off her neck into a chignon. "What do you think?" she had asked her husband. "Suit yourself, Rosamunde," he'd said. His response satisfied her. The silver hair around her face warmed her coloring and made her look elegant, grandmotherly, kind, though she had come to realize, but not without regret, that there would be no grandchildren.

The stranger brought from his inside coat pocket a pair of horn-rimmed glasses and read aloud the description of the drawing: "*Clive Adams, Writer, Beverly Hills, 1953*. Theobald was in his early twenties when he made this sketch."

"I should say."

"Wait'll you see the later portrait of Adams. Just down the way," he said, pointing in its direction with his thumb.

She recognized in the stranger's face and voice qualities she liked: quickness, openness, and a willingness to please. His boyish face was eager, friendly. Though older he resembled her son, Whitacker. The resemblance lay in the light-colored, expressive eyes, the long, dark eyelashes, a wistfulness. Curious, but too reserved to ask, she wondered if the stranger had been attracted to her because he saw in her a resemblance to his own mother. The ease of their dialogue reminded her of the casual, good-natured exchanges usually reserved for strangers seated together in an airplane. She enjoyed the cordial impersonality of anonymity and the temporary freedom of casting off a routine role. In this brief encounter, she'd play neither wife nor lover nor mother nor poet.

"I missed the grand opening of the exhibit," she said, noticing that the guard had removed himself from his seat at the door and vacated the hall. "I would have liked to have seen the artist in person. There are plenty of his self-portraits here."

"I posed for Larry Theobald," he said all of a sudden, his eyes widening.

"Really?" she said in a noncommittal manner.

He nodded. "No lie! Would you believe?"

The excitement in his voice reminded her of the time when her son, then a ten-year-old, came home with Joe Montana's autograph after a Forty-Niners victory.

"Me. A nobody!" He made a broad gesture with his hand, and they both turned in unison to acknowledge opposite them a row of paintings of famous celebrities who had posed for Theobald.

"You must have been very excited having been picked to be among such elite company," she said.

"Excited? Let me tell you!"

"How did it come about?" she said, engaged by his story, responding to his tone of self-congratulation.

He smoothed down his tie, adjusting it. "Some years ago, I ran into him at City Lights Books. Theobald was in San Francisco with Clive Adams—his mentor, as he called him." He interrupted his story, and beckoned to her enthusiastically, indicating that he wanted to show her something at the far end of the room. She followed, quickening her step to be in stride with him. They moved by a row of small pen-and-ink portraits, stopping at a large portrait in vivid acrylics. He pointed to it. "Ta-dah! The centerpiece of the exhibition."

She stood for awhile, observing Theobald's painting of a big, raw-boned man. The writer Clive Adams, in old age, painted a year before his death, her acquaintance told her.

The figure's stark isolation was accentuated by the salon's incandescent lighting. In the painting he wore a velvety-black turtleneck sweater, which emphasized the sanguine-colored complexion, his hawk-like nose and sharp features. His hands rested in his lap, rigidly clenched. Especially arresting were the intensity of his Viking-blue eyes, the steady frigidity of his gaze. How strained and taut his facial muscles seem, she reflected.

"He looks like he's in pain," she said. "Arthritis."

"I didn't catch that," her acquaintance said. "I just thought he looked tormented like any writer."

She was quietly amused that he thought all writers were tormented souls.

"He was a lot sprucer when I saw him. Like I said," the man continued anecdotally, "I was in City Lights one evening and Adams, here, was signing autographs for his new book, *Alpine Journey*. Well, Theobald asked me if I ever came down to L.A. I told him occasionally I did a business trip. 'Call me,' he said. 'You've an interesting face, interesting hands.' Theobald spoke in this affected British accent. He's American-born, Larry is, but he acquired his accent having lived so many years with Clive Adams." He quieted his voice to a confidential whisper. "His long-time lover." His whisper was muffled by the static stillness of the room. She would have liked to have let in the crisp, autumnal brightness that lay outside the museum walls.

"Yes, I know about that. Now Theobald is the mentor to a young man. So goes the world," she said resignedly. A line from an Auden poem ran in her head without her willing it. One word in it troubled her. Lay your sleeping head, my love, human on my faithless arm. But she spoke matter-of-factly to the friendly stranger. "When I was a student at U.C.L.A.,

Adams was a resident guest writer one semester. I would have liked to have taken his class, but I couldn't fit it into my schedule. Theobald often drove him to campus."

"Yeah? Anyway, Theobald was very interested in hands," he said, spreading his own. The side of his right index finger bore stains from nicotine.

"You modeled for him?"

"Sure. Why not? I drove the Coast Highway out to his home in Malibu," he said, accentuating *Mal*.

"Was Clive Adams there?"

"No, he was away. We were alone in his studio. The only other person on the premises, I believe, was the Chinese houseboy who let me in." He deliberated slowly as if wanting to recall a detail which had escaped him. "From his home you had a fantastic view of the Pacific." He made a broad, sweeping arc with his hand. "I'll bet you'll never guess what happened afterward?" he said boyishly.

She looked at him curiously, wondering why he felt compelled to relate the event so carefully to her. "After you posed for him?"

He cleared his throat and coughed. She could smell his dead, stale tobacco breath, which seemed to her such a private disclosure between strangers.

"Afterward," he said, pausing as if he wanted to make sure of all of his facts, "afterward, I left my glasses behind in his house. My glasses!" he repeated incredulously.

"Oh, I know how helpless I've felt when I've forgotten to bring along my glasses," she said. Often her son had told her that without his glasses he felt naked.

"Not so much helpless at that point as foolish," he said. "I stopped at a gas station and telephoned him, I'll never forget. You know what he said?" He paused and looked at her with an ingenuous expression. "I hear him say over the phone in his clipped British accent, 'You can pick them up in the mailbox.' That's what he said. Well, how-do-you-do! 'You can pick them up in the mailbox.' "

She felt caught off guard. How humiliated the poor man must have felt having been so indifferently used. Her first impression of him had been correct. He was naive, basking in a moment of reflected glory. Then the old, worried argument between poets came once again to her mind: What is better, innocence or experience? In her youth, she had argued hotly for experience, and now she wondered if innocence weren't the better after all.

She smiled awkwardly at the man and shrugged, leveling her sympathetic hazel eyes toward him. "So. Do you have the drawing?"

He shook his head, "Oh, no! As far as I know he still has it in *Mal*ibu." He shrugged it off, then glanced down at his watch, drawing away from her. "I must be off. Nice talking to you. Enjoy your visit in our fair city."

She smiled at his assumption that she was a tourist. "Palo Alto," she called after him.

"Hey, let's hear it for Palo Alto! Go, Cardinals," he said making a fist and raising it in a cheer.

He made her aware of the time, reminding her that her husband might be walking through the Fruitless Mulberry grove toward the De Young from the Hall of Science. They had settled on going their separate ways for about an hour, then meeting again in the museum's coffee shop. Later on, after their son closed his insurance office, they would join him for dinner at Masa's, a San Francisco restaurant known for its fine French cuisine. Whitacker was bringing his partner for them to meet.

"Mom, can you try to understand?" Whitacker had said. "Guy and I are going to make it together. We have a home. We love each other."

"Whit, the only thing I've ever wanted is for you to be happy," she had replied.

Rosamunde felt apprehensive about this meeting, troubled by her own ambivalence. Monty took the news on the cuff. His resilience was a blessing. "We would have liked it to be different," he had said, putting his arm around her closely. "But it's his life, Rosie. We can't live it for him. I hope they're happy."

She watched two young men come into the empty gallery hand in hand. Together, she thought they set a startling composition. One had fiery, unruly red hair; the other, an Afro-American, wore his hair in long, neat cornrows. They seemed, as far as the world could tell, a happy couple. She thought of her son and suddenly felt alone and vaguely sad. Was he truly happy with his life's companion, as he called him? A question that hung in her mind as a continuous source of worry.

Rosamunde recalled coming home early one afternoon after holding a poetry seminar at the university, while Whit, then a senior, should have been in his high school classes. She'd heard giggling coming from Whit's bedroom. Hysterical, drunken giggles. She recognized her son's voice. The other voice, a male's, was unfamiliar. Her heart had felt as though it were pounding in her ears. She knew then what she had already feared. In blind ignorance, she had recriminated herself asking over and again helplessly: What had gone wrong? How had she failed? In stealth, she had left the house and driven away in her car.

The following fall, after Whit had left for college, he telephoned her from his dormitory. "Mom, I brought my old glasses by mistake. I forgot my new prescription ones. Could you mail them to me? I think I left them in my bedroom. On top of the bureau or maybe in the drawer of the nightstand."

She remembered going into Whit's sunny room with its pungent scent of orange blossoms and cinnamon incense. She'd looked about his bedroom for his glasses. She couldn't locate them at first. Then she had opened up a drawer to a maple nightstand. She had found them in their case lying in plain sight. Underneath them lay old letters, photographs. Guiltily, she'd snooped. She couldn't help herself. Photographs. Her son and a male friend had taken turns taking each other's picture. Whit had borrowed a dressing gown from her wardrobe, make-up from her vanity. Ashamed of herself, yet human, she had stared at her son's picture, startled by what she saw. His lips were a ruby red, the lipstick filled in fuller over his upper lip, his cheeks rouged the color of pomegranate. He had lain posed on his bed, odalisque-style, in her silk peignoir, an anniversary gift from his dad. How she had loved the luxurious softness of that silk—and knew Whit must have too—with its print of forest blooms and a cockatoo in flight on bright-green wings. She hoped if Whit were ever to know of her indiscretion, he could forgive her shortcomings.

She sought distraction from that pain of memory and regret and surveyed the gallery once more, glancing at the portraits, taking stock. They seemed to her a social registry of mostly Hollywood celebrities, famous, if not rich: writers, producers, directors, painters, photographers, actors, actresses, singers, artists. Some she recognized by sight—Bette Davis, Wray, Lang, Mapplethorpe, Olivier, in ennui and loosened tie, and a former governor of California. For shame, Larry Theobald! You're a snob! And what else I don't know, she thought.

Leaving the exhibit, she hurried down the vaulted, cold hall, which reminded her of a mausoleum, and turned into the museum gift shop. Before joining Monty, she'd have just enough time for a browse and a trip to the ladies'.

She looked at the display rack of new books and picked out one in a plain beige cover, *Male Nude Drawings*, by Larry Theobald. Leafing through the pages, she looked for an interesting face. But the interesting sketches, she discovered, were not the ones she had viewed already in the special exhibit hall. The line drawings in Larry Theobald's *Male Nude Drawings* were from the portraitist's secret life, printed by his permission from his private collection, sketch after sketch of the male form in homoerotic poses, standing, sitting, recumbent. Some of the nude models were in their thirties, more of them appeared to be in their early twenties, all were anonymous. At first she stared unabashedly at the obvious, her interest captured at first by prurient novelty—an unknown face, torso, a penis captured in repose or erect. Was one of them the stranger who had been her guide in the exposition hall? Within these pages, she had found no David, nothing ideal nor heroic. Her curiosity abated, she became thoughtful. *What are these to me? Yet what of that poor, gullible man, leaving behind his glasses, dismissed like a servant?* Feeling uneasy for dawdling and keeping her husband waiting, she returned the book to the display rack.

A few minutes later, leaving the ladies' room, she passed again by the gift shop on her way to the museum's cafe. A man was at the counter, his back to her. She recognized his dark brown jacket, and knew he was the acquaintance she had made in the exhibition gallery. As she hurried along her way, she saw that he was speaking enthusiastically to a clerk. He held in his hand a beige-covered book, perhaps even the same one she had examined.

The line from the Auden poem went around and around in her head again. *Lay your sleeping head, my love, human on my faithless arm.* She thought of Whitacker and his lover and changed the key word to *faithful*.

Vincent

When I opened the letter from my friends Bertrand and Stuart, a pressed flower wrapped in tissue paper fluttered out. I hastily checked the return address and was not surprised to find they had moved again, this time from Dorset to West Sussex.

> The house we purchased last September is all quite lovely. Bert says that in the spring it will be beautiful: violets, primroses, bluebells, rhododendrons, anemones everywhere.

I recognized Stuart's flowery, secretarial handwriting. He does all of their personal correspondence, much of the housekeeping, and all of the driving. Even though Bertrand was a navigator in the R.A.F. during the Second World War, he's never cared to maneuver a car. Since their return to England, Bertrand studies and writes philosophical discourses and putters about in their rose garden. They have had this domestic arrangement for well over forty-five years and have not been separated from each other since the war.

> I must be peculiar, though. Yesterday the wind blew

and the rain lashed the windows until they looked like sheets of weeping, wide-open eyes, open but sightless. Gulls swooped and screamed in defiance of the wind, which blew them about like paper kites unable to control their flight. Today there's a clear blue enamel sky, and I long for it, with all the rain of winter, yet it makes me vaguely sad.

You asked me in your last letter if I've been painting landscapes. Not really. My heart's gone out of it. I am sure we made a tragic mistake ever leaving the United States. I should never have left California, far away from where my lovely dog, Vincent, lies buried. You may think me silly, I don't care. Scarcely a day goes by, if ever, that I don't think of him. Sometimes I can talk about him, especially, of course, with Bert. But sometimes I can't share his memory—some things are best left unsaid even when we know them—I am not ready now or ever to say goodbye to him. Never.

I sigh, recognizing Stuart's nostalgic regret and a familiar pattern with them of restless uncertainty. Following Bertrand's retirement, they left the United States twenty years ago, and have resided in six different countries and more than ten different houses, delusively hunting for a happy belongingness they think they left in their native land.

Despite the instability of their address, I am certain one habit remains inveterate. Their tea time, wherever they may be, is promptly at four o'clock as it was while they resided in Saratoga when I was teaching with Bertrand in years past. God forbid that tea be delayed a dot! I picture Stuart setting out biscuits and a stack of thickly buttered toast and marmalade, then adjusting the cozy on the pot of steeping jasmine tea, just as he did the first afternoon that I was invited to take tea with them. At four o'clock, then as now, I can imagine Bert eating voraciously, taking up piece after piece of toast in his small, chubby fingers.

On that afternoon, I drove Bertrand home from the high school in San Jose, where we both taught English, to the long narrow driveway about the Montalvo Estate and turned up a small lane to their large, airy California ranch-style house on Mendelsohn Way. Stuart, whom I had met only briefly once before, came out on the porch and greeted us.

"Oh, you did bring Arabelle," he called. "Good for you, Bert. Come in, come in, Arabelle. I am so glad you're here. A young woman like you must have many things to do."

Stuart smiled drily and, it seemed to me, self-mockingly, as he drew himself up to his full height. He was tall—elevated even more by Italian-made shoes with two-inch heels—and slim. His slick black hair was tied back in a ponytail. In spite of his sharp, upturned nose, he reminded me of a caricature of Rudolf Valentino. He impressed me on that first occasion as being vain and disdainful. But that was a facade to protect him from slight and rejection, as I was to learn later.

As I stepped onto their threshold, a massive Dalmatian bolted toward me. He nosed my buttocks and encircled me. Then all fifty muscular pounds of him lunged for me from behind. His great paws grappled my thighs. The jolt of his heavy body dislodged one dangling earring of the pair I was wearing. It flew off and landed on the Oriental rug.

"Down, Vincent Two, down," Stuart commanded quietly as Bertrand rushed over to help me find the displaced earring, which had blended with the paisleys of the rug.

The beast snarled low in his throat and then backed off meekly and sat obediently at Stuart's side.

"I hope I'm not seeing the telltale signs of jealousy," Stuart said, giving Bertrand a meaningful look. Then Stuart addressed me in an unruffled tone. "Did he give you a start? I rather suspect that you get on with dogs. You do, don't you, Arabelle?"

"Yes, I like dogs," I replied, attempting to regain my composure, still shaken by the dog's attack. "Why is he called 'Vincent Two'?"

"It's a long, sad story, Arabelle," Stuart said. "Somewhat connected with Vincent van Gogh. I'd rather not bring it up now."

"No, nor I. Still, I've never seen Vincent Two behave like that for any of the fourteen months we've had him." Bertrand said, shaking his head apologetically in my direction. "And we brought him home as a puppy."

"I can assure you, Arabelle, he'll be quite the gentleman once he's settled down to his tea. Won't you Vincent Two, old fellow?" Stuart said, stroking the back of the dog's neck. Having reassured me and Vincent Two, Stuart took from the tea cart a porcelain china bowl and filled it with tea and some milk, stirring into it four lumps of sugar and set it before Vincent Two, who lapped it up daintily.

"He has a sweet tooth," I commented nervously.

"He wouldn't be a proper Englishman if he didn't," Stuart jested.

After the dog was humored, teatime resumed. Bertrand offered me a chair. I selected a straight-backed one across the room from the black-spotted dog. Still unnerved, I defensively pressed the chair firmly against a wall of mahogany bookcases. Stuart handed me a cup of tea without sugar while the dog, having finished his, crouched down at Bertrand's feet, his head resting on large, crisscrossed paws.

I was aware of a transmogrified id fixed upon me, behind the stare of coal-black eyes. While he trained his gaze on me, I looked away from him to the fussy collection of ceramic Dalmatians, arranged in formation across the length of the long mantel of the fireplace.

When I had finished my cup of tea and excused myself from an offered refill, having fulfilled what I thought was required of a short, polite first-time visit, I promised at Stuart's insistence that I would come back again another time.

The next time I drove Bertrand home after an English Department meeting, he related an anecdote about Vincent van Gogh, Stuart's favorite artist.

Van Gogh's mother gave birth to a son who died in infancy. That son had been christened Vincent. A year to the date of his death, a second son was born to the van Goghs, still in mourning for their firstborn. They named their second son Vincent.

"Sounds like something out of Grimm's fairy tales," I commented.

"Yes, rather like. Not too long before we owned Vincent Two, Stuart lost a beloved Dalmatian he had named 'Vincent' after the painter. They were with each other every moment. Inseparable. At supper Vincent lay under the table at Stuart's feet. During the night, he slept at the foot of Stuart's bed."

"He sounds like Stuart's alter ego."

"You might put it that way, I suppose. The sad part came when Vincent was nine years old. Suddenly he became lack-luster, unable to move without great effort. There was nothing the vet could do for him. Nothing we wouldn't have done. Dr. Kennedy told us Vincent had been born with a congenital defect. Arteriosclerosis. He died beside Stuart's bed, too weak to get up on it. March twenty-ninth at ten minutes past nine in the morning, I'll never forget. We both suffered his loss. Far, far the worse for Stuart, though. He wept for the loss of his soul mate day by day. Lamented month upon month, those heavy days. At length, I gave Stuart another Dalmatian puppy. We both agreed on calling him Vincent Two."

Tea that afternoon took a course that would become routine. The dog growled menacingly at me when I entered the hallway, and Bertrand held fast to his chain collar, restraining him until the dog lay down and I was assuredly seated. It may have been Stuart's idea to have Bertrand invite me in the first place, for, as soon as tea was over, Bertrand excused himself, his tall, portly figure quietly withdrawing to his library study. Padding behind him, close by his heels, was Vincent Two, unmistakably his dog. Then Stuart and I would go outside and sit together in their rose garden.

One afternoon Stuart guided me out to the garden through his bedroom, which smelled of fresh linen and delicate lavender. As we stepped through it toward the French doors that led outside, I caught sight of two studio portraits on a dresser. One I recognized as Greta Garbo; the other was a young man with a sleek-looking, Valentino-style haircut. Propped up next to the studio photographs was an enlarged snapshot of a Dalmatian dog.

"That, of course, is my lovely Vincent," he said, leaning down and tapping an edge of his dog's picture.

"Were they alike? Vincent and Vincent Two?"

"In name only, I'm afraid. For me, a world of differences, loves apart. Bertrand wanted Vincent Two to be mine. But, from the very start, there was no denying he was Bertrand's. And the plain truth of the matter is I don't mind a bit. My lovely Vincent trotted beside me everywhere. Any place. I wouldn't dream of leaving him behind. He jumped into the front seat of the car. Off we'd go. I'd take him off the leash, wherever. Never a bit of trouble. When we got where we were going, say the art supply store, I'd give him the car keys. He'd hold them in his mouth and wait for me outside. If approached by some stranger, just dandy. He'd be polite, but reserved. He'd allow himself to be petted. But he never went out of his way. Never a licker, either. Never the beggar."

Then, noting my sidelong glance at the other photographs and sensing my curiosity, Stuart pointed to them delightedly. "Yes, Arabelle. Isn't Garbo beautiful? That's Cecil Beaton's portrait of her. I've seen *Camille* hundreds of times, and shall again if I can. Cecil Beaton gave me a dried damask rose allegedly worn by her."

"Do you still have it?"

"It deteriorated, petal by petal, to dust," he said, brushing his hands across his graying temples, glimpsing himself briefly in the mirror over the vanity. Then he turned to the companion picture. "That's me, or what was me, for a wonder. Ancient history, you know. I thought I was destined for a great career in films. Now then, let's go outside. I want to have a chat before you leave."

We sat in the patio. Near us, in a cunning wicker cage, a cedar waxwing stood. He had one crooked leg. Two seasons before, the bird, drunkenly dazed from feeding on the spoiling berries of a pyracantha hedge, had beaten his wings against the stained-glass panel on their front window and injured himself. Stuart had taken him into the house, cleaned him up and mended his wing and broken leg. As we talked, we could see a flock of the waxwing's brothers, who had returned for a week to this enclosed garden in Saratoga, a stopover during their migratory flight to Mexico. A wild rush of yellow and brown wings riotously lit into the pyracantha bushes. We watched them as their beaks pecked furiously into the fermenting red berries.

Stuart raised his voice to be heard over their shrieking clamor.

"You always strike me as a young woman with lots of vitality."

I smiled self-consciously as he continued.

"More so than I can say for Bertrand. He's phlegmatic. Didn't used to be. I owe the change in him to the death of his mother. She gave him the push he needed. We dreamt of coming to the U.S. She told him in no uncertain terms: 'Do it. You'll regret it always if you don't.' His parents, my Aunt Olga and Uncle Charles, took me in after my parents died. I could have done worse. They were very good to me. And I a poor member of the family tree, at that."

"How old were you, then?"

"I was nine when my dear mum died."

He paused and looked sadly at the caged waxwing, then continued speaking. "How is Bert at school? All he finds time to do over weekends is read students' papers and talk of retiring one day to Surrey."

"Surrey!"

"Yes. That's become his great dream. Certainly not mine. Why would I want England's dismal rain and depression when here I can feel the sun on my back?"

"I hope you don't have any immediate plans to return to England."

"None at present, I am most happy to say. Still, I'll admit the idea is often hanging in the air."

"The kids at school adore Bertrand," I said, returning to his earlier question. "They make a play on his name, 'Thistleton,' and call him Mr. Mistletoe. Of course, not to his face." I thought of his rotund, sanguine-complexioned face with the wreath of silver and ginger-colored curls about his pate and laughed aloud affectionately as did Stuart.

"Yes, he knows that, and rather likes it. But what I'm getting at is, does he talk to anyone apart from his students? He says little at home."

"He doesn't say very much. Except about department stuff."

"That doesn't surprise me. He's a solitary bachelor at heart. At best, his mother, my Aunt Olga, understood him. You know, he told me he likes the way you've taken hold. If he said that about me, I'd take it as a compliment. Which I'm sure he means. He says that you are reading the part of Juliet with him for an English literature class. That was his mother's favorite play. He had a line from the tragedy inscribed upon her stone: 'An untimely frost upon the sweetest flower.' Well enough! You'll do Juliet very nicely, I should think."

"Why, thank you, Stuart. I really don't mind reading. But I get the jitters at first when I have to go on a stage."

"Really understandable, I think. Every actor has the jitters until he loses himself in the role, forgets the audience. I once played Richard," he said, holding up two fingers. "And not too bad, so I've been told," bringing his long, nervous hands about his shoulders as though he were draping a royal purple and ermine mantle about them, turning his profile to me in a sentimental pose.

"Bertrand remembers Edith Evans in the role of Juliet."

"As Juliet? Nonsense! Evans was the nurse. Bert imagines. Oh, how I wish for all that he imagines that he would let himself go, but I suppose he can't stand the levity."

I told him of the time when Bertrand had come to my

classroom before my sophomore students entered for the first period of the day. While we figured out what changes in the class scheduling would be for an assembly taking place that morning, a bird darted between us, his wings like a feathered rainbow. My startled fingers reached up, and, fluttering between them, was a hummingbird. I let him loose outside the door. I'd wanted Bert to be as surprised as I was, but he'd just "hmm'd," nonchalantly.

"Yes, that's so like him. Never one to express his feelings openly. I'll tell you," Stuart said, changing his emphasis and pointing forlornly at the wild cedar waxwings feeding in the hedges. "They are beautiful, but distracting. Because of my poor caged one, I'd like to see them fly away."

His mood shifted abruptly from the plight of a broken bird to his own complaint. "Bertrand is so silent sometimes, his silences so oppressive. He marks his papers all weekend when there's a whole continent to explore. Oh, I suppose it's selfish of me. He really doesn't have to work, you know. He was born with a good, solid, brass spoon in his mouth, but he never took to the family meat-packing business, Thistleton and Ritter, sausage makers since 1875." On pronouncing "sausage," Stuart squinched up his eyes in distaste. "I suppose it's just as well that he enjoys teaching. Well, there you have it! Are you getting chilly out here? Before you leave, I'd like to give you something."

We reentered the house, this time by way of a little laundry room, converted into a studio, which smelled of oils and turpentine. Wrapped canvasses were lined up against the walls.

"Are you getting ready to exhibit?" I asked.

"I thought I might bring up a few things to show at Montalvo," he said, unveiling a little landscape. "It's a typical English country scene. Some of the buyers seem to like my acrylics and chocolate-box cottages and copper beech and plane trees. I often get a handsome price for them. But I have something different in mind for you." He opened a portfolio and pulled out a pen and ink sketch of a Dalmatian standing alertly at attention. "You don't have to take it if you don't like it."

"I do like it, Stuart. I'll hang it in my bedroom."

"You really will, now?"

"Yes. Thank you. I do like it. But won't you miss it?" I asked, aware of his loss, touched that he would give me a likeness of Vincent.

He gave me a quick, searching look, then smiled sadly. "Oh, I've more of those. I've drawn him from memory dozens of times. I could do it blindfolded. Mind you, I want the frame back. Take your time on that. I'll need it back if I draw that size again."

I was unable to return the frame as soon as I would have liked as Bertrand did not set a time for tea for several weeks afterwards. Only occasionally did I catch a glimpse of Bertrand's comfortable, portly frame entering swiftly into his classroom next door to mine. Nor did he appear in the cafeteria at lunchtime, first in line with a tray of food, as had been his habit. I thought if he wanted my company, he would come out of his shell sooner or later. Finally, though, when he hadn't spoken to me in a long while, I saw him striding past me in a school corridor. I caught up to him. He continued walking, humming underneath his breath. I tugged gently on the sleeve of his sports coat. He stopped humming, and slowed his stride.

"I know you are there, Arabelle," he said. "I have things on my mind. Please, don't be offended, but I can't bear anyone to touch me."

And he continued on his way, leaving me open-mouthed and stupefied, and, despite his apology, hurt by his curtness. I recalled Stuart speaking of Bertrand's lapses into oppressive silences.

Occasionally, during those several weeks without face-to-face contact, I overheard his lectures to his students. His emphatic accents stressed the sheet-rocked walls that separated our classrooms. Then, one morning, he stood briefly at my classroom threshold before students arrived. "Tea?" he said simply.

On the drive to their home, Bertrand told me Vincent Two had turned vicious." A neighbor girl rang the bell, selling Girl Scout cookies. When I opened the door, Vincent Two flew out at her before I could restrain him."

I gasped. "She wasn't hurt?"

"Yes. Very shocking. He lunged at her. Knocked her down. Bit her in a nasty way on her legs and calves. The girl was terrified. She cried for her mother. I had gotten Vincent Two in control, but still the house was in an uproar. We were all frightened. The police had to be called, of course."

I murmured my sympathy. "How is the little girl?"

"She's all right now. But one laceration on her leg required seven stitches. We can't apologize enough to her or her family. Vincent Two went berserk, that's all I can think," Bert said, shaking his head glumly. "I had to make the decision to put him down."

What a pity, I thought. Though I had been afraid of Vincent Two, he was a handsome dog.

"Stuart opposed me, would have none of it. 'Family's family, good days or odd. You keep to the family,' was what he said." Bertrand cleared his throat. "I made a mistake giving Stuart another Dalmatian dog after the death of his beloved, gentle Vincent. His Vincent should have been the one and only. I've caused us no end of trouble."

During that afternoon's teatime, the sense of tragedy surrounding their household was palpable. Stuart thanked me for returning his frame, saying, "I could never have replaced it."

I put Stuart's letter aside, and unwrapped the flower, the tissue paper rustling between my fingers. It was a snowdrop, turned to the color of ivory, slightly browned along the edges of its pressed petals, the flower hanging like a bell from its hooked stem. It fit perfectly on the palm of my hand. I contemplated it for a moment. As February begins to turn to spring, the first snowdrops pierce the barren earth with their pure white flowers. As delicate as they look, like ballerinas that have been waiting in the wings, if they like their home, they are about as tough as a plant can be. Then I carried it into my bedroom, where years ago I'd hung Stuart's drawing of Vincent One, and laid the flower on top of the frame.

Raccoon

Barbara pulled her truck into the front yard of her summer house late in the afternoon of a hot July day, and we were met by milkweed, and skunk weed, and the stirring, wiry whir of crickets. She called this place in St. Thomas in the Missouri Ozarks her "getaway." Situated on two-hundred acres of scrubby pine and cleared, dry grassland was a weathered, one-story farmhouse in need of a fresh coat of paint. The entrance door was shaded by a small pitched roof, supported by posts, one on each side of the cement step. Further up the gravel drive, west of the house, stood the big, old barn, whose exterior, like the house, had turned to a silvery shade of brown.

The children, all under eleven years, my one and Barbara's four, piled out from the back of the truck and made a beeline toward the barn. They were anxious to show my daughter the old-fashioned surrey Barbara had bought at auction and kept in the barn, the eggs in the dovecote, the climb up to the hayloft. After touring the barn, they'd explore the pasture and bring along empty coffee cans to dip for pollywogs in the unstocked trout pond.

The children waved to us before they disappeared behind a hedge thicket of wild blackberries. Soon afterwards, a tall, lanky youth emerged from among the high, dry weeds with a .22 rifle in hand. As he came closer, I saw that he was about sixteen or seventeen, his head close-shaven like a fugitive from justice.

"Rick," Barbara greeted enthusiastically.

His sunburnt face, coal-black eyes, and craggy features made him look strangely familiar, perhaps someone I'd met in the past.

"This is my friend from California, Ava Howard. She and her daughter are visiting this weekend. Ava, meet Rick Thomas."

"Nice to meet you, Rick. Been hunting?"

"Uh-huh," he said, poker-faced. "Coon. I didn't know you all be comin' up today, Barb."

"Ava," she said, after giving Rick a meaningful look, "I told Rick he could hunt coon on our property as long as the kids and me weren't on the premises," Barbara said.

"Understood," Rick said.

"I've never seen a coon," I said, trying to make conversation.

"How come you know Barb?"

"We went to high school together. In East Los Angeles."

"Oh," he said, turning his attention from us to some vantage point toward the woodlands.

Through Barbara's letters, I had formed some secondhand knowledge of many of her neighbors in this Ozark community. The Thomases of the hamlet were all decedents of the original settlers of St. Thomas. Rick Thomas' parents and younger brothers and sisters lived on some poor farmland a mile and a half down a washboard road from Barbara's farmhouse. Rick's mother, June Thomas, sold eggs from her home, tended a truck garden, cared for her four younger children, and babysat for others. Her husband worked as a hired hand.

Barbara led Rick and me, grocery sacks in hand, into the kitchen, the main room in the farmhouse.

"As you can see, Ava, furnishings, Early Distress, mostly stuff I've bought from Goodwill or the like. It'll make do for now."

"Cozy," I said, glancing about me and looking in at the overstuffed couch and oak chairs in the little sitting room off the kitchen.

"Rick, lay the gun on top of the refrigerator," Barbara said. "Out of reach of the kids."

He did, and then sat down on the kitchen floor, his back and almost bald head leaning against a wall, all six feet of him in patched worn jeans, his body hard, lean and sinewy.

"Have a seat, Rick," Barbara said, motioning to a chair next to me at the kitchen table.

"This'll do fine," he said.

Then she began sweeping the linoleum with a broom she had brought in from the rickety front porch.

"How's your family?" Barbara said. "I've got to catch up with all the news I've missed since I was here last month."

"They're okay."

"Your mother?"

"June's same. Mean as ever," he said without emotion.

"You mean she's busy," Barbara said, translating his taciturn answer. "Well, I know she has her hands full what with taking care of your littler brothers and sisters and the farm. Ava, June does all her cooking on a wood stove. Even heats water on it for bathing Saturday nights. The Thomas children all come to Sunday school well-scrubbed, neat, and clean."

Every time Barbara mentioned his mother, Rick's expression grew hard, guarded.

"How's your dad?"

"Same. Easy come, easy go."

"Any new calves since I was here last month?"

"We lost one. Stillbirth. Strangulation," he said, apparently taking morbid relish in reporting this event. "Choked on its own cord."

His answer was disarming though at the time I couldn't have said why.

"Too bad. Had any luck hunting?" Barbara said.

"Nothing much."

"What do you do with raccoon?" I asked.

"Some folks eat 'em. Taste sort of like lamb," he said, making a face in disgust. "Would gag a maggot. I just kill 'em dead. That's if I can get away early enough. June keeps me hard at it. Choppin' wood. She's always pussy-whippin' me with somethin' I gotta do or other. 'Rick, I've got my hands full'," he said, pitching his voice high in a mock-female voice, " 'I can't do hit all myself.' "

"Rick," Barbara said, her voice suddenly sharp. "I don't want to hear that kind of crude talk."

He mumbled under his breath.

I felt anxious for Rick to leave, so Barbara and I could have our own conversation. With the children around, we really hadn't had many private talks.

"You've had a haircut since I saw you," Barbara said.

He scowled.

I was surprised when I saw that she had stopped her sweeping and was regarding Rick with a friendly smile. I had forgotten about her infuriating habit of talking to every casual acquaintance, a careless friendliness bestowed evenly with strangers. Now, as in high school, she looked wholesome, bosomy, auburn-haired, and freckled. Her hands, wrapped around the broom handle, were large and capable.

"It'll grow back. At least for now it'll help you keep cool," Barbara said, her voice a honeyed patter.

"June done it," he sneered, not hiding his contempt. "Snipped off my sideburns 'n' all. She damn near scalped me alive," he said sullenly moving his hand to the top of his bald head. "All's I know, soon's I turn eighteen I'm headin' out. Joining the Marines."

Barbara stopped talking, and the room became quiet. The air in the kitchen was static, heavy as hot breath.

Then Rick looked from one of us to the other with eyes sleepy lidded and brooding.

"Where 'bouts in California?" he said to me. "Maybe I'll be sent out to Camp Pendleton."

"San Jose."

"That anywheres near San Diego?"

"No, we're north. Near San Francisco."

Rick yawned in an exaggerated way, stretching his arms high over his head, as he rose to his feet.

He glanced again at me. His look was intimate, disconcerting. I felt as though I couldn't conceal my squirming. I wondered what Barbara saw in this sulky, ill-tempered, uncouth adolescent. My thoughts reverted to my first impression of Rick. I knew now why he seemed familiar. He resembled Al Verona, a guy Barbara and I had known in Los Angeles. From the eighth grade until she quit school in her senior year, she had gone steady with reliable, safe, "C minus" Norman Nickols, who eventually became an air-conditioning engineer. Then, midway into her senior year, she quit school and broke off with Norman. She took up with

Al Verona, a street-wise dealer, a version of Rick Thomas. But some years later, she married Shelby Fairchild, an engineer very like Norman.

"Do you fish in the river, Rick?" I said, out of politeness, wondering if he were ready to leave, not wanting to detain him if he were.

"Not much. Well, sometime," he drawled. "I get catfish."

"Big?"

"Oh yea. You can pull out ones big as you please. Fighters. They can whip their weight'n wildcats," he said, stretching his arms way out.

I smiled in spite of myself at that moment, his turn of expression delighting me. As was common with people in these parts, Rick said "kin" for "can" and "jest" for "just," and bit into his *R*'s hard, distorting the vowels that came before them.

"Big 'n' ugly. You can fry 'em up real good. Hey, Barb, bum a cig?" he said, suddenly pleased with himself. She tossed him one, which he caught in mid-air, while she herself lit up another. He reached in his jeans pocket and brought out a wooden match and struck it on the bottom of his boot.

He took a long drag from the cigarette, inhaling deeply and exhaling calculatingly, deliberately out of his mouth, the smoke rising up to his nose, then curling up to his nostrils—French inhaling, puckering up his ripe, almost girlish, sensual lips.

"Would June let you go with us tomorrow in our canoe? We'll row down the Osage pretty much all the way. Stop at a sandbar and let the kids swim," Barbara said.

I was irritated. Here I'd come all the way from California, and she was lavishing all her attention on this rube, whom she could see as often as she came to St. Thomas.

"Depends on what the old lady wants of me," Rick said, picking up his gun. "What time?"

"Eight thirty or nine. As soon as we get the kids dressed and ready. I'll call your mother. Maybe she'll let you."

"Okay. You just do it," he said turning toward the door.

"If your mother lets you, we'll pick you up. Bring a fishing rod. You can show Ava how you catch catfish."

"Ya wanna?" he said, turning to me with a crushing charm, drawing on the end of his cigarette slowly, then offering it over to me, his hand raw and calloused, all of his fingernails bitten down to the quick. I waved it away, and, in this motion, some hairs on his arms grazed my skin.

His "Ya wanna?" startled me. I sensed what had drawn Barbara to Al Verona and to Rick: a brutish sexual energy, libido's raw self! In my junior year in high school, I'd accepted a ride home in Al's primed Chevy. He'd said he was on his way to Barbara's. He sped off the main highway without warning and drove his car into a walnut orchard. The next sensation I felt was his hard muscles pinning me down, forcing me, and dust blowing in through the open windows.

We looked for a moment out the open door as Rick walked down the driveway carrying his gun nonchalantly in the crook of his arm. Little dust clouds formed at his heels as he kicked at the gravel.

Barbara said, "I'll call June Thomas right now." She lifted the receiver from the wall phone. "Oh, it's busy," she stage-whispered to me. "Party line. Neighbors gabbing."

Then she spoke into the receiver. "Hi, Mrs. Wenzel! It's Barbara—Sure, I'd recognize your voice. And Mrs. Campbell? That you?—Yes, the kids and I are—Fine, Fine. My friend Ava from California is here with her daughter. Nope. We didn't bring our husbands. Shelby's holding down the fort in St. Louis. Yea, ah huh. Did Mr. Wenzel tell you he'd drive us to a downstream branch of the river? Good. Yes, we've brought the long canoe. We'll all be down at your store in the morning. Just one more thing. You say you're calling June Thomas?—For quilting.—I wonder if you'd ask June to call me after you've talked to her. I want to ask her if Rick can go canoeing with us. Oh, that so? Okay. Well, all right. I'll see you and Mr. Wenzel about nine tomorrow."

"I guess you heard most of it," she said, replacing the receiver. "Mrs. Wenzel said she means to call June for the quilting group. She'll give June my message. Anyway, we've got kids to feed. Beds to make."

"Now, what can I do?"

"You can cut up the watermelon. Help me make sandwiches. Kids'll be coming in soon," Barbara said, taking out loaves of bread from a sack of groceries and then opening the refrigerator and bringing out peanut butter and strawberry jam.

"Make me five sandwiches." Barbara said, as we stood side by side at the kitchen counter. "Tomorrow I'm going to eat all day. Being that Shelby's not around nagging me to diet." Barbara slid out a wooden breadboard from just underneath the countertop, and I laid the slices of bread on it.

"We'll bring hot dogs, too, Ava, remember how I loved your mother's salads?"

I looked into her smiling, rosy face and nodded, reminded of how in high school she had liked being asked to stay for family dinner at my house.

"I don't think my own mother ever made a salad in her life. I've always envied your being so thin," she said looking at me appraisingly. "Anyway, I know where there are bunches of watercress growing along the riverbank. We can make a bitchin' green salad."

"Sounds delicious!"

"Mrs. Wenzel doubts June would let Rick off for an entire day. We wouldn't be back by suppertime. If then. June doesn't have it easy. She was a Winkleman before she married John. Fifteen. She's about our age. There's always been bad blood between the Thomases and the Winklemans."

"How come?"

"A stupid feud."

"I thought that kind of thing happened only in the movies."

"No, it's true. Goes back to their great-grandparents fighting over some property line, I've heard. In these parts, you can probably find a Thomas behind every rock. And fewer Winklemans. Anyway, John's folks have never really accepted June as one of their own. Rick sides with the Thomas clan. That makes June the odd one out."

"I've never heard any guy refer to his mother as 'pussywhipper.'"

"Yes, that was bad, I agree. Rick thinks he's a man. Doesn't want to be bossed around like a kid. June expects Rick to carry his weight. All her kids have chores."

"Well and so do your kids, and so does mine. That's no excuse to call your mother a 'pussywhipper.' June works hard, I'm sure she doesn't deserve to be called names."

"June says he's got a hair-trigger temper like all the Thomas clan. I've never seen any of it. Not full-blown anyway."

"You think it's only teenage rebellion?"

"Yes. He'll straighten out. At his age I acted pretty crazy, dropping out of school and all."

"I was thinking about your old boyfriend Al Verona just today." I paused. Al Verona hadn't fit into our conversations or correspondence until now. I'd never told Barbara about the incident in the orchard. At the time, as a teenager, I'd felt too ashamed to tell anyone. In my struggle, Al had released his grip on me only when I'd sunk my teeth down on his ear so hard, I'd sprung the wiring across my braces. *I'd whipped my weight 'n wildcats.* "Rick reminds me of him."

"Does he?" Barbara sounded curious, amused.

"Yes. And I don't believe your young barbarian can be civilized. Anymore than Al could."

"Civilizing Al was the farthest thing from my mind. Al and me, we had a fast sweet time. But I'd never have been proud to call him the father of my kids."

I put the knife into the peanut butter jar and faced her squarely. I spoke very slowly, as I do when I want my daughter to take heed and be careful. "Al could hurt people. I think Rick is capable of hurting people, too. I think Rick would seize every opportunity to be cruel, just as Al did."

Barbara looked reflective, and nodded soberly. She was looking out the window over the kitchen sink, as though she were peering into the distant past. "Al bragged to me once—" She stopped in mid-sentence, turned to me, and touched my shoulder tenderly. I felt on the verge of tears, but held back. Here I'd been looking forward to having her sole attention, and now I had it in a way I hadn't predicted and wouldn't have preferred. "I'm sorry," she said. "I am so, so sorry." Then her voice took on a hard edge. "That Al Verona was the biggest prick in town."

The next morning, driving toward a downstream branch of the Osage River, at least a good mile away from Wenzel's Groceries, Herman Wenzel at the wheel of the Dodge truck, Barbara and I sitting up in the front seat, the five kids and their collie and the canoe in the flatbed, I asked, "Barbara, what about Rick?"

"Oh, goddamn it, Ava, I forgot all about him!"

"But how could you?"

"I don't know. I had too much on my mind. I guess I got distracted."

"Shouldn't we turn around? Go back and get him?"

"We should, but I don't think we can. It's too late for that. It's already ten o'clock. We've made a late start as it is," Barbara said. "Besides, we don't even know for sure that June Thomas said he could come."

"True enough. We don't."

"Also, he can't swim. None of the Thomas children can swim."

"So?"

"So probably just as well that he isn't coming along. I made a careless mistake including him."

I agreed but didn't say anything.

We shrugged him off or tried to. For the present, I felt little guilt and much relief.

It was dusk when we returned to the farm. The kids, sunburned, tired, lay asleep in their sleeping bags in the back of the truck. As Barbara and I approached the house, I saw something dark in front of the door and looked to Barbara anxiously.

"Barbara, what's that?"

Barbara looked at me, and I knew we were both thinking the same thing—whatever it was, was no gift left by the welcome wagon.

We stepped out of the car apprehensively, picking our way with rapid, cautious steps to the porch. What it appeared to be, at first, was a bulky shape, strung up by a rope over the doorway. We looked with amazement at each other.

Before us, hanging upside down by its long, bushy tail, was a large, gray-brown creature, surely over two feet in length. As if in effigy, its heavy body dangled face-downward.

"Ugh!" I shuddered, and stepped backwards.

Barbara moved past it and flicked on the outside switch for the porch light. We looked at its face at close range. A mask of black fur surrounded the eyes and pointed nose.

"What in God's name?"

"A raccoon," Barbara said. "Shot dead. Clean between the eyes."

I stared at it, speechless at first, aghast. Its monkey-like hands had stiffened, turned inward as if in prayer.

"Jesus!" I said.

"Yes, God-awful, and all the more so. Her teats look full of milk. Her kits, wherever they are, must be starving," Barbara said.

Between the penitent paws lay a scrap of paper rolled up like a cigarette.

Barbara plucked it out, unrolled it, and we both read the message scrawled in pencil. There was no mistaking its author.

City Girls
This is coon

"God, he's insane," Barbara said, her face indignant, angry. "Bastard! What got into his head?"

"God only knows. His way of getting back at us for leaving him behind?"

"I think you've got it right," Barbara said, setting her jaw hard, lowering her eyes momentarily. "Now, let's be quick about it before one of the kids wakes up. We've got to cut her down, carry the body out back to the dump." She rushed into the kitchen returning with a knife and a sheaf of newspapers.

The phone was ringing when we returned to the farmhouse from our grim mission. Barbara answered the alarmingly sharp rings.

After what seemed like a long minute, she drew in her breath and sighed into the receiver, "Oh, my God! How?"

Then she listened attentively until the caller finished a message.

"That was Mrs. Wenzel," she said.

"What's happened?"

"June," she stammered. "June's dead."

"How?" I asked in disbelief, trying to grasp the weight of her words.

"Rick was cleaning his rifle after coon hunting. It went off. The bullet hit June in the chest. Accidently."

"His own mother! How horrible!" I could still feel the stiff, dead weight of that mother raccoon in my hands. We'd wrapped her in newspapers, taking pains to be quiet so as not to wake our children. I imagined he'd been careful, stringing up that rope, knotting it around her tail, writing his note. Perhaps he'd even hung around for a while afterward, out of sight, waiting for our return so that he could see our reaction. I shuddered again. "Barbara, I don't believe it was an accident."

"But he was cleaning his gun," she repeated. She fumbled in her blouse for a cigarette.

"If Rick knows anything, he knows his own gun." I moved

to the sink to wash the gray newspaper ink smudges from my hands. The small window over the sink was as glossy black as a pool, reflecting my face and part of the room. But in my mind, I could see clearly all over again Rick walking away from the farmhouse, scuffing at the gravel in the driveway. How handily he carried his gun in the crook of his elbow, as though it were as much a part of him as his arm. "He can claim it was an accident."

She sank into one of the kitchen chairs, then lit her cigarette and inhaled, considering. "You may be right. Mrs. Wenzel said the sheriff didn't arrest him. His father's standing by his story." Barbara slapped the tabletop with the flat of her hand. "Rick'll get away with it, too. Damn it all! I should have made the effort to get him this morning."

"And if we had, what then?" I remembered how relieved I'd felt when we'd left him behind, and knew I wouldn't have felt safe with him.

"Then June would be alive, now."

I watched Barbara smoke her cigarette, flicking the ashes into an ashtray. She looked like an older, wearier version of the selfsame girl who'd pursued Al Verona. "Yes, she'd still be alive. And Rick would still be hating mothers."

We couldn't have saved June or civilized Rick. What we could do, what we did then, was take care of our own children. We went outside and carried in the sleepyheads, one by one, from the night.

Emily

"Bury it there," Daddy's mama said, as she jerked her hoe free of milkwood weed and pointed an upraised steel blade toward her freshly rousted seed rows. "Do it now before I turn the hose on and run it down the row. You've got lots of other pretty dolls," she said, looking angrily at Emily, cradled in my arms. "That one is ugly. I told your father I'd put your mother up in my house 'till he found work, and I told your mother to take that doll away from you. I didn't want it in my house."

I laid Emily down on the earth and began to dig like a dog. My bonnet strings had become undone and trailed wet sand down my cheeks.

"Here's a trowel. Use it. Not your hands," Daddy's mama said, as she stooped down at my side. "Let's tie up your bonnet before you lose it."

I put Emily into the hole I had dug for her, and her chocolaty smile blended into the earth. I covered her over with mud and stuck bonnets of pink, blue, and violet sweetpeas into the mound I had built.

"She doesn't get a Christian's prayer 'cause she's from a heathen race," Daddy's mama said. "But you did a real nice funeral."

Daddy's mama's backdoor slammed, and I heard Mama call for me. I ran to her and buried my face in her stomach. She smelled of sleep.

"Mama, I've lost Emily," I said.

"How in the world?"

I fidgeted away from Mama, and looked down at her flimsy alligator heels. One of the straps around her ankles had peeled loose, and she didn't have nylons on.

"Where have you been playing?" Mama asked.

"Daddy's mama and me had a funeral. We buried Emily."

"What's that child telling?" Daddy's mama said, coming up from behind us.

"Mrs. Davis," Mama said, "have you seen Shelley's doll, Emily?"

"Phew," Daddy's mama said. "I haven't seen that nasty thing."

"I can't believe Shelley would lose it. She clutched that doll from Greyhound bus to Greyhound bus all the way out from Atlanta to California. Did you and she have a home burial for her?"

"I'd slap my child good if she told such a thing. I'll tell my son on you, if you say such a thing. We did no such thing."

Daddy's mama's smooth white face wrinkled. I could not see her blue eyes.

"My son was to marry Lily. He gave her a diamond dinner ring. He never gave you one. Jew women look pretty, but they don't hold their bloom."

Mama took my hand. Her nails pressed into my palm. Her alligator strap trailed on the ground.

"Come, Shelley," she said. "Show me where Emily is buried."

I took her to Daddy's mama's garden plot. We searched

about for a marking place, a mole-mound of earth, the bonnets of blossoms. All the rows were level. All the freshly seeded rows had been hosed down.

Mud and Strawberries

Several summers after her father died and Laurel was five, her mother rented a large Victorian house in Oakland on Underhills Road. Laurel loved the shape of the house, and she liked to count its four stories, including the cellar and attic. It was too big for two people, Mrs. Robbins said, and she intended to rent the upstairs bedrooms to Presbyterian missionaries of her church.

Even though Laurel liked the clean naphtha and bready smells in the enormous enameled kitchen and butler's pantry in the main part of the house, it was down to a room in the basement where she went every day. It had been the owner's study and was shaped like the inside of a very large shoe box. High on one side were oblong windows that were never opened. They were splattered with mud from rain-splashed geranium beds outside and they let in only slanting bits of light.

The room had a very dark smell, which Laurel sensed was a man-smell, dark as whiskers and sulphuric-smelling as the odor left in the air after a wooden match is struck.

Its walls were covered with racks of pipes, guns, and elks' heads. One end of the room was filled with many leathery books, gold and checkerboard red and black. On a heavy mahogany desk lay a heap of pens and pencils and some stacks of yellowish paper. There was a tilted globe of the world, black-lined, green-patched, light orange, and pale blue in color, which Laurel liked to spin and swirl on its axis. It made a squeak as it went round, and if she twirled it fast enough, it made a whistle.

Over the thick-woven rag rug Laurel would go exploring. The rug was splotched with tiny cakes of queer-smelling mud. She supposed the mud splotches had been made by someone, probably a man, who had tracked back and forth on the carpet. There were also minute pockets of mashed-up ashes, and an occasional bit of cigar leaf. And there were many coarse, yellowish hairs, evidently from the hide of some tail-thumping dog. If her cheeks brushed against the hairs as she crawled about, she felt as though she had come in ticklish contact with a man's whiskers.

Under the corner of the desk Laurel found a torn section of paisley cloth from what might have been a lady's sewing satchel. It made her think of her mother and the stout, dark-dressed ladies who sat together in the same pew on Sabbath mornings. But except for that piece of cloth, the room was completely a man-smelling, dimly lit room.

Her mother disliked the basement room. She didn't intend to use the room, she said, and wouldn't have it cleaned. She couldn't understand why Laurel wanted to play there when the sun was bright outside and the garden was full of summery flowers and butterflies.

One day, four ladies from Mrs. Robbins' church came to lunch. Laurel was too small to help much, but she had been instructed to carry out a single task. When the main course had been cleared away and the table was bare of everything but the linen tablecloth and napkins and the remaining silver and flowers in the center, Laurel was to bring in the dessert.

Laurel's mother had set six glass bowls of strawberries, each bowl on a white plate, on a ledge in the butler's pantry. Mrs. Robbins was to say, "Laurel, now you may bring in dessert." Laurel was to walk then through the swinging door to the pantry, lift one plate with both hands, carry it, carefully balancing, back through the swinging door, and place it in front of a guest. She was to go in and out of the door six times, setting the sixth bowl of strawberries in front of her own plate.

As planned, after the lunch Mrs. Robbins cleared everything away. She brought a silver tray containing a basket of small fruit cakes and a cut-glass bowl of powdered sugar and set it on the sideboard. She then lifted the sugar and cream to the linen level of the table, and set the basket of cakes by the flower centerpiece.

Laurel awaited the command. The five grown people's heads stuck up on long waists high from the table, and their glances slanted down upon Laurel at an angle, just as the light slanted down into the basement room from the skypatch beyond the geraniums.

"Laurel, now you may bring in the dessert," Mrs. Robbins said.

Laurel went through the swinging door and surveyed the six bowls of strawberries sparkling on the pantry ledge. They were exact, prepared, and waiting for her. The berries were moist from careful cleansing and round and red, redder than the geraniums. Each bowl was heaped symmetrically, so that each dish of strawberries looked identical to each other pile.

Laurel marveled at the skill with which her mother had divided the strawberries. When she herself had been called upon to divide a handful of candy jelly beans into only two equal mounds, she had great difficulty in getting them even.

Yet here were the strawberries, larger and more variously formed, in indistinguishable delicious mounds.

Laurel felt her tongue sparkling and moist like the strawberries. She plopped one strawberry into her mouth and tasted it. The pink juice dribbled down her chin onto her starchy white pinafore, and she swallowed quickly. But the loss of the one berry destroyed the symmetry of the bowls. So, hastily, by taking one berry from each of the five other bowls, Laurel leveled them off again.

"Laurel," her mother called.

No time for eating the other five berries. Slowly Laurel began walking, carrying the bowls. Balancing them through the swinging door was like going on tiptoe. It was pleasant to set a sparkling bowl importantly before a grown-up and be gazed upon with smiles and gratitude.

At last there remained only Laurel's bowl, and the five large strawberries that lay on the pantry ledge. Laurel gathered up the five and worked them teetering onto her bowl. They looked as if they were going to topple, but they stayed in place.

When Laurel at last put down her own bowl, all six persons were ready to eat. Each person lifted her spoon, and the cream and sugar went shuffling from hand to hand.

The company of ladies became silent, their faces seeming hot with the reflected color from the glass and strawberries. And the mother's face flushed reddest of all.

When the guests had gone, Mrs. Robbins led Laurel to the basement room and locked her in—to let her reflect on her greediness, she said.

To be locked up alone in the room she had loved for its queer, secret smell of mud and hairs was now a punishment.

A rage at her mother seized Laurel, so that she snatched

the yellow papers from the heap on the mahogany desk and crumpled them and tore them, scattering them every which way on the floor. She knocked several pipes down from the pipe rack and beat upon the locked door with one long-stemmed pipe until its bowl was broken.

Then she lay face down on the rug and cried until she could cry no longer. But a large ache remained within her like an empty lung which could no longer be filled by the secret quality of the room she had destroyed.

The Wedding Dress

The little girl, Delia by name, watched her mother hem doll clothes on a portable Singer sewing machine set on a table in a corner of their home, the manager's cabin at the Green Lantern Motel. The mother, who was herself doll-like in stature—scarcely four feet, ten inches tall—liked to work with miniature-sized machinery and cutlery. Before she had begun hemming, she had cut out the doll's dresses from calico cloth remnants with round-tipped scissors her daughter had borrowed from her third-grade teacher. Then, with small, freckled hands, the mother spread out each finished, wrinkled doll piece on Delia's toy ironing board and pressed the clothes with a diminutive, electric iron. When she finished, she handed Delia a doll dress, warm from the iron, and sat on the cool blue linoleum floor with her legs crossed and then wound up a yellow and black toy locomotive engine Delia had long ago outgrown and discarded, idly watching it spin about in circles on the floor. Delia felt left out and alone. She didn't know what her mother would do next. Occasionally her mother spoke of the Warsaw ghetto, a strange, faraway place of her childhood. Oftentimes the mother fell into long spells of silence.

This time, though, after the toy engine wound down, her

mother spoke. She told Delia about taking a real train from Grand Central Station in New York City to Southern California's Imperial Valley.

"My papa carried my suitcase to the train. 'Nettie, don't go,' my papa said. 'Change your mind. Mama and me don't want you to go. Why do you marry a man we've never met? A boy you don't know? *Dir abesher vedir shtrosen*.'"

When Natalie Harper said "Papa," she began to cry. She hugged herself with her arms and rocked back and forth.

"I miss Papa. I miss Mama. God is punishing me. *Got shroft mir*."

She began to shudder and tremble and cry, sitting forlornly for a period of time with her arms across her breasts, her head low, moaning desolately and mumbling broken phrases in a language her daughter could not understand. Delia did not know what she could do to make her mother feel better.

She went to her father. "Mother acts funny. She wants her mama and papa."

"I know," he said, nodding his head glumly in agreement. "It doesn't look good."

Frank Harper, Delia's father, was worried not only about his wife, but also about other matters. That winter, usually the busiest tourist season in the desert town of El Centro, motel business was slow. He had not been able to rent out most of the Green Lantern's cabins. Eight of the ten were vacant.

One morning Delia stood by her father's side as he locked up the two Texaco gasoline pumps, which were in front of the motel's registry office, directly off State Highway 8.

"Delia, I'm driving out of the valley to find work. I don't want to leave you. But I can't see any other way. Will you be a good little Indian while I'm out? Mind your mother?"

She wasn't sure exactly how he meant for her "to mind," but she nodded her head "yes." Then she looked up at his dark-complexioned face, so like her own, and asked timidly, "How long?"

"Thirty days. Tops. I'll give you a nickle for every day I'm gone. How much is that?"

"One dollar and fifty-cents."

"Correct," he said, shaking her hand. "You've got a deal."

He left a handwritten sign on one pump, which read:

NEED GAS?
GO TO CABIN #1
WIFE HAS KEY.
FRANK L. HARPER, OWNER

"You're a dead duck if you run out of gas out in the desert," the father told Delia.

The next morning before sun-up, from within her room behind her parents' bedroom, she heard the flush of the toilet, followed by running water from the shower pipes in the bathroom. She listened to the footfall of boots as he stirred about in the cabin, and, after a time, the sizzle of bacon frying in the kitchenette. She smelled fresh coffee and hot grease. Then, as he prepared to leave the cabin, she heard her parents' muffled goodbyes to each other. In the darkness of her room, she lay awake and listened to her father starting up his car, backing it out of the carport, the engine groaning as he drove out of the courtyard toward the highway.

He's leaving to be a carpenter, she thought. He had told her he would find work outside the Imperial Valley. He'd drive as far as Barstow or Needles or even cross over the California border into Arizona and take whatever carpentry work he could find. Riding out so far from home, after day's end, he'd lock up his tools in his handmade chest and park his car along the side of a stretch of highway in the desert and curl up to sleep in the backseat of his Chevy, his loaded rifle near him on the floor of the car.

During the month her husband was away, Natalie Harper, who feared the heat of the sun and blamed it for her frequent headaches and nausea and faintness, tried to keep her daughter inside their cabin. If the mother gave her permission to go outside, she made Delia wear a sunbonnet for protection against the harmful rays of the sun. Delia thought she looked like a baby in the bonnet, and, as soon as she was out of her mother's sight, she loosened its ties about her throat and let the cap fall back from her silky, brown braids, slide down to her shoulders, and slip to the ground in hasty abandonment.

Freedom was a liquor to her spirits. Whenever her mother lay down for a nap and she heard her mother's sighful breathing, Delia seized the moment and stole out of the cabin to escape from the oppressive silence and loneliness within the four walls of the cottage.

One long, hot afternoon, Delia watched from a window of Cabin Number 1 for the occasional movement of vehicles on Highway 8 as they passed by the Green Lantern. She counted two sluggish International Harvesters, and, after many humdrum minutes, a rusty Mack truck. So uneventful were the signs of movement, that she lost count of the cars coming and going down the road past the motel toward town. A nervous blowfly buzzed in frantic darts from one to the other of the window screens. She wanted to swat it, but she didn't want to rouse her mother, who had fallen asleep in a straight back chair. As soon as she heard the steady rhythm of her mother's quiet breathing, Delia acted quickly and made her escape out the front door on rapid tiptoe. Then she ran off toward the dump site behind the motel where she hoped to meet with playmates to play "wild horses" or "mustangs gallop, buffaloes butt."

Delia found two little sisters, whose parents were renting Cabin Number 10, sitting on the ground, eating their lunch under the shady oasis of the beefwood trees near the dump. Recognizing Delia, each handed her a thick, cold wedge of salty fried potato.

All of a sudden, as she swallowed down a soft lump, she felt a sharp tug on her braid, and looked up in surprise to see the frowning face of her mother, who had wrapped up her fiery, coppery red hair under a black scarf.

"Didn't I tell you it's too hot to play outside? Naughty girl."

Delia rose up from the dirt pile where she had been sitting, and accidently scratched a shin against the broken spoke of a discarded bicycle wheel. Embarrassed, she winced, her eyes smarting in pain. She didn't want to behave like a baby in front of the sisters with whom she had shared a snack.

A trickle of blood ran down Delia's leg, and her mother noticed the red scratch.

"Good. There. You see? God has punished you."

Delia's face burned with shame. In haste, she turned her back to the little girls without saying goodbye.

Her mother's words planted in her a fearful anxiety she felt she could lessen only by some magical ritual.

Delia hung behind her mother as they walked back to their cabin. She stopped momentarily at a cluster of oleander bushes, closed her eyes, and picked at random a handful of flowers from among the long slender leaves, whose tips felt as brittle and sharp as fingernails. She imagined that the dry leaves were witches' fingers and the moist, scarlet blossoms would turn into poisonous apples she dare not eat.

At six-thirty on a dry, sultry June morning, the red mercury column in the large Coca-Cola thermometer on the front building of the Green Lantern Modern Motel already registered seventy-eight degrees. Frank Harper drove his family in the old green Chevrolet out of the pea-gravel courtyard of the motel and headed the car toward El Centro and the Southern Pacific railroad station, where his wife, Natalie, would board a seven o'clock train bound East toward New York.

Delia sat beside her parents in the middle of the front seat, sandwiched between her mother on one side and her father at the steering wheel. Natalie Harper was going away on the train in the same brown silk dress she had been married in ten years before by a justice of the peace in Yuma, Arizona, a border town known for its no-waiting, quickie chapel weddings.

Delia loved brushing up close to her mother's side, feeling against her bare arms the silky coolness of the brown dress with its rich cloth-of-gold weaving. Once, when Delia was five, her mother allowed her to play dress-up in it. Before she was quite aware of his presence, her father had come into the cabin, found his camera, and made ready to take a picture of her. He had crouched down behind her, almost level with her height, as she posed in front of a long, vertical mirror. She was taken by surprise when she realized she was being observed by her father, having caught a glimpse of his form and a shadowy reflection of his high-polished, black-leather cowboy boots in the glass in front of her, and she whirled around and faced her admirer. He snapped the camera at a perfect moment. The photo captured a blushing, beaming Delia, disarming and mischievous, her back to the mirror, standing teetering in her mother's brown suede dress pumps, adorned in the borrowed finery of the elegant silk dress, a plush, scarlet-red velvet hat pushed back impishly from her head, framing her cherubic face.

This morning the dress revealed the richness and charm of its past. Natalie Harper sat on the worn leather seat of the car, her figure slight, her face pallid, the brown high heels she wore barely touching the floorboard. More than once she kissed Delia's cheek or fidgeted in and out of her purse. First she fished around at the bottom of the bag for a hairbrush and comb, and bringing them out, drew the brush through Delia's long brown hair, still tousled from sleep. After rearranging Delia's hair with the comb, Mrs. Harper finally replaced and clasped a red barrette at each side of her daughter's hairline. After she finished grooming her daughter, she reached down again into the purse and brought out her ticket and checked and rechecked it.

As Frank Harper drove the automobile down the highway toward town, a long-tailed, flighty roadrunner crossed the road with her brood of chicks, and he slowed down and swerved to the right to avoid hitting them. They passed a neighbor's field of rippling alfalfa. The dry, medicinal smell of earth and root, fragrant blossoms, and purplish-green high grasses mellowing toward harvest under the hot, desert sun drifted into the passenger windows of the old Chevy.

In a voice pitched high enough to be heard over the sound of the motor and the wheezing rattle of the muffler,

Natalie said, "Oh, just smell the clover. Ralph's got a big crop."

Frank slowed the car down and turned his face sidelong as he pointed his left thumb in the direction of the pasture, and then at his wife.

"Stick around. You'll see me mowing. Ralph'll need help bringing it in."

Delia felt frightened when her parents argued with each other and acted as if she were not present. At the motel, when they quarreled, she could always escape and wiggle away out of sight. But here, enclosed in the moving car, there was no exit, no escape, and she drew her breath in tightly. Not until she felt the soothing movement of the silky sleeve of her mother's arm stretching way out across her to her father's shoulder and up the back of his neck did she relax and begin breathing regularly again.

"Frank, please. We've been all through this," Natalie Harper said, as she drew her fingers through the coarse, brown hair and stroked the back of his neck.

At first her touch on his back made him stiffen as if he were caught in hurt surprise, but as she continued caressing him, he relaxed his guard, and he grinned boyishly in spite of himself.

Frank Harper had tried to understand his wife's sadness and loneliness, her depression—her sense of disorientation expressed bewilderingly in Polish and Yiddish phrases and fragmented stories of her early childhood in the Warsaw ghetto. He did not comprehend her nostalgia for her parents, the Malachai family he did not know, who had emigrated from Poland to New York in the early thirties. Since Frank came from the ancestral stock of North American English settlers, followed later on by generations of prairie farmers, frontier pioneers, his wife's experience as a twentieth-century Eastern European immigrant was wholly foreign to his understanding. He was absolute and final on the matter of Delia. On no account would he ever permit his daughter to accompany her mother to New York on a visit of long duration or one that might prove permanent. He was adamant in his objection despite the fact that grandfather Isaac Malachai, his wife's father, had sent money for full rail fare as well as for a child's half fare. He would never let Delia be taken away. Besides, as long as Delia remained with him, there lay the possibility of his wife returning—for better or worse, in sickness and in health, vows he had not taken irresponsibly.

At the Southern Pacific railroad depot, there were only a handful of people standing on the station platform waiting to board the train or wishing a friend or family member "Godspeed." Taking a passenger train for a long-distance journey coast-to-coast was already in decline, but Natalie was afraid to fly and had insisted she would travel only by train.

Frank helped his daughter and wife lift themselves up to the steps of the train to the sliding door of a passenger car, which a conductor held open for them. Then Delia walked behind her mother and father in single file as they made their way through an almost empty train until her father, who carried her mother's suitcase and overnight case, located the appropriate seat assignment and stopped and put the luggage in an overhead compartment.

He reached into his trouser pockets for loose change and gave it all to his wife for tipping. Just at that moment a whistle was blown as a last warning call for boarding.

Natalie kissed Delia goodbye and reminded her to obey her father. The child felt a twinge of guilt and wondered if her mother were leaving her behind because she had been a bad girl and disobeyed her and played outside in the sun. Not wanting her mother to see her tears, she wiggled away from her mother's embrace, and stared out a smudgy train window, where she caught sight of a short-haired, yellow dog foraging about by a trash can on the long wooden railroad platform. She glanced back over her shoulder only once and saw her mother and father parting.

Frank Harper seemed awkward and shy even though he towered over Natalie. She took his hand in hers and said:

"Do you remember when you first met me at this station? I thought you were a Mexican. I'd never seen such a dark, sunburnt man."

He bent down to embrace her, and they wrapped their arms around each other until the train jolted and jounced and forced their separation.

After deboarding the passenger train, father and daughter stood hand-in-hand together on the long railroad platform and waved farewell to Natalie Harper, who gazed out at them tearfully from a train window. Then they caught a last glimpse of coppery, red hair before the locomotive lurched and plunged forward, gaining momentum and moving out of their sight into the silence of the desert.

Often, thereafter, Delia listened during the night for the whistle of a locomotive blowing not far off from the Green Lantern. Sometimes she heard a coyote bay in answer. As she lay in bed in the darkness of her room, the click-clacking train rumbled over the railroad ties, and the vibrating rhythm rocked her back to sleep.